Bob Moats

Doyle's Law

By Bob Moats

Doyle's Law

This is a work of pure fiction. Names, characters, places, and incidents either are the product of the author's imagination or are used fictitiously, and any resemblance to actual persons, living or dead, business establishments, events, or locales is entirely coincidental.

ISBN – 978-0-9960634-6-3

For information and address:
Magic 1 Productions
P.O. Box 524, Fraser MI 48026-0524
Website: http://murdernovels.com
Cover design by Bob Moats

Extra special thanks to:

Special thanks to Val Brooks who edited this book and for all her great suggestions.

Thanks to the pre-beta readers Cindy Gross Valstad, Susan Haughton, and Al Norris.

Thank you for purchasing this book. I hope you enjoy it as much as I enjoyed writing it for my faithful readers. If you liked the book please feel free to write an honest review on the product page where you got this book from. I'd appreciate it. Please feel free to email me to tell me what you thought about my stories. I love hearing from the readers. I can be reached at murdernovels@bobmoats.com thanks again!

Doyle's Law

Chapter 1

Doyle stood silently on the rustic wooden porch of his secluded cabin in the woods just north of the Metamora State Recreation Area. It was very early in the morning as he gazed at the fog that hadn't quite lifted off the waters of Lake Metamora - breathlessly displayed in front of his cabin. It seemed to hang in the early morning air, wistfully swirling in the slow moving wind from the north. The air had a slight chill, as it always had early in September, just before the leaves of the trees started to wither with the impending cold. Their show of fashionable autumn colors were a favorite attraction for the tourists who came wandering through the forest to admire Mother Nature's handiwork.

Doyle wasn't happy to be here at his cabin right now, he would have rather been in the city doing his job. He didn't take the news well when he'd been told that he was put on suspension from duties for unnecessarily roughing up a suspect in an attempted mugging. Doyle was a fifteen year veteran homicide detective for the Detroit Police and was waging an internal war against the crime and corruption he saw in his duties as a cop.

Last weekend he was accused of being excessively rough on a suspect at the scene of a mugging. He was minding his own business as he circled his car around Grand Circus Park down in the heart of the city, when he witnessed a woman being dragged into an alley. He pulled the unmarked car to the entrance of the alley and got out, spotting the perp beating on the woman. He ran around the car and entered the alley yelling at the man to cease his attack.

The alley was a one-way. No exit at the back, so the suspect had nowhere to go but through Doyle. This didn't make Doyle happy as the man dropped the woman and charged him. Prior to his time on the force, Doyle had spent ten years in the FBI's Terrorist Task Force. He had extensive hand-to-hand combat training, so this perp wasn't someone he was worried about. Which is where the suspension came in. The suspect ended up in the hospital with multiple contusions, broken ribs and bones, along with several cuts and bruises from being pummeled against the brick walls of the restaurant next door to the alley.

Doyle was surprised the perp hadn't carried a gun, but the hunting knife he wielded was no problem. Doyle brought his arm and shoulder up under the man's arm and twisted it, causing the man to drop the knife. Doyle then spun the man around and brought his elbow to the man's jaw. The man wouldn't go down and kept fighting, which made Doyle angry, so he utilized his tactical skills to stop the perp's attack. Doyle had noticed lately that his temper was getting worse the more he had to deal with the criminals he put up with every day. The lowlife in the alley did nothing to brighten his mood.

"Art," came a pleasant female voice from his right, just off the path to the road out front of the cabin. He was lost in his thoughts and hadn't heard the car drive up, which annoyed him for not being more alert.

"Hey, Gwen. You snuck up on me," he responded.

"You mean to say I got the drop on the famous Arthur Doyle, detective supreme? How is this possible? You never let people surprise you."

"I was lost in my thoughts of how I could have handled myself this last weekend. Before putting a criminal in the hospital. My anger is getting worse and I'm afraid I'll really hurt someone one day." He looked out at the water, taking his eyes off the attractive woman. She was Doyle's girlfriend who put up with the man more than he deserved. He often wondered why she was attracted to him. He was decent looking, sure, in a rough sort of way, but he was moody and sullen most of the time. He knew how to have fun, but usually when he was drinking.

"Before you really hurt someone? You put the man in the hospital and he was injured bad enough that the legal defense lawyers went after you with a vengeance. I'm surprised the Captain just suspended you with pay for two weeks. It was good he told you to get out of town so the mess would go away." She paused to look out at the lake. The fog was lifting and the water was as still as a sheet of ice. "It was all they could do to keep the press away from you. I know your mouth moves much faster than your brain sometimes. When it comes to criminals, you just have nothing good to say."

"There is nothing good to say about the assholes. They're all scum and lowlife morons who deserve to be beaten within an inch of their wasteful lives." He turned to her and smiled. "I'm sorry, I really hate it when the criminals are getting better treatment than the victims. Who mourns for them? I'd like to become a vigilante and run around in a black ninja outfit smiting out vengeance on the trash that lurks around the city."

"You'd be a cute ninja. But, that isn't the answer."

"Don't start with the 'justice for all speech' again," he said sharply. "There should be no justice for those people. They don't show mercy or justice to the women they rape, beat and mutilate do they? They don't stop and think that they shouldn't pull the trigger on a father whose kids are watching, just to get the man's wallet and money. And, the gangs that, just for kicks, beat the crap out of a young couple minding their own business, coming from a movie - did those criminals think about justice when they did that? Hell, no! There is no justice with these animals."

7

Doyle's Law

Gwen decided not to get him angrier than he already was. She knew where his breaking point was and she had to calm him. "I got word today that I was accepted at Rash and Hunt. I'm finally going to be a lawyer at a prestigious law firm."

Doyle hated lawyers, which was the one sore spot in their relationship. He always held his tongue when it was mentioned. "I'm happy for you. You worked hard to get there and I knew you'd do fine."

"But?" she asked.

"No buts, I'm happy for you. Really." He stopped before he might say something he'd regret. He was already upset with his life at the moment and didn't see the sense in lousing up his love life, as shaky as it was already. Gwen had worked hard to get the position she wanted badly. He was really happy for her.

"Look, to show you that I'm glad for your new job, I'll take you to dinner."

"On you? You're paying?" she said with a grin.

"I always pay. When was the last time you paid for dinner?" He slowly moved to her, and putting his arms around her shoulders, he placed his lips on hers and gave her a long kiss.

She didn't fight the kiss, she gave into it. One thing Doyle could do well, besides take down criminals, was kiss. It usually melted her into submission for anything he wanted. Usually, it ended in the bedroom, or on the floor in front of the fireplace.

He suddenly backed up when his cell phone rang out the theme from "Jaws," which always annoyed

Gwen. He looked at the caller ID and said, "It's the Captain. Why the hell is he calling me?"

"You won't know until you answer," she replied.

"I don't know if I want to talk to him." He finally put the phone to his ear and answered. "Doyle here."

"Doyle, you already know who this is, so I'll get to the point. I need you back here as soon as possible," the captain said into his ear.

"What? Has crime run rampant without me?"

"Don't be a wiseass, Doyle. You have friends in the FBI and I need you to work with them as quickly as possible. You are going to be our liaison between us and the feebs."

"Okay, what's the deal?"

"The mayor's two children have been kidnapped and their nanny was murdered. The threat has been made on the mayor's life and we are getting a task force together with the Feds to work on this. I need you to handle the Feds. Get back here as soon as you can." He hung up, which pissed Doyle.

"I've been summoned back to the city. Seems someone took the mayor's children, murdered the nanny and are threatening the mayor."

"What do they want?"

"Dickhead didn't say, he ordered me back and hung up. It would serve him right if I didn't show."

"Art, think about the children," she said softly.

He paused, feeling conflicted. He wasn't happy with the way things were going with his job, yet Gwen was right. If he could help get the children back, it was something he had to do.

"Okay, I'll get my things and head back down to the city. I'll talk with you later and explain everything I find out."

She gave him a kiss and turned back to the path to her car. Doyle went in the cabin and picked up his still-packed bags. He didn't bother to unpack them, which worked out fine in this situation. He carried them to his cherry red Dodge Charger parked in the front of the cabin. He looked down the road leading out of his property, watching the cloud of dust from the dirt road made by Gwen's sensible Prius. He hated that car, but made allowances for it.

He went back and closed up the cabin and stood one last time on the porch looking out to the lake. "This is where I want to retire to. Maybe after this situation."

*

Chapter 2

Doyle drove out from his property and over to Lapeer Road, heading south. He had time to think about his life as a cop during the one hour drive back to Detroit. He enjoyed the job, at least when he started. Now, he was hating it more and more. Crime was getting worse, lawyers were getting the criminals off with loopholes in the law, so arresting them was a joke. There was no justice for the victims and the defense lawyers made the victims look to be the instigators of the crime. It was getting harder to have the victims testify in court if the lawyer made them look bad. Plus, the suspects often threatened the lives of those testifying to get them to drop charges. Once, it had felt good getting criminals off the streets, now it seems as if he were spinning his wheels. What was the point?

Doyle finally reached I-75 and jumped on the freeway. He carefully maneuvered into traffic; he didn't want his car involved in a fender bender. Traffic was heavy for the time of day, he went with the flow, staying away from the nutcases on the road. A car flew by Doyle and had to be doing over ninety. Doyle was doing the seventy mile an hour speed limit and it griped him when people sped. They usually didn't get there any quicker than those doing the speed limit, due to traffic. Their recklessness only served to make the ride on the road more dangerous for others.

He arrived at the border of Detroit and got off at Eight Mile Road, heading east to his apartment. He knew they wanted him there quickly, but he wanted to change and pick up his extra gun. He pulled down Harper Avenue and up to the building where he made his city home. It was just inside the city limits of Detroit to keep the brass happy, but just barely in the city, keeping Doyle happy.

He moved quickly to change his clothes, and strapped on his Sig Sauer handgun in the quick release holster riding on his left side under his arm. He liked it better than the holster clipped to his side on his belt. Easier to hide and prevent a perp from pulling it away from him. Then he put a smaller .38 in the special holster clipped inside the belt at the back of his pants. He put on his jacket and straightened out his tie. He hated ties, but it was a part of the uniform for detectives, ordered by the brass. Made the detectives look civilized, according to some psychology genius who claimed to know what the public expected from their police force. Hell, he thought, the public didn't give a rat's ass about what they wore. They were hated in either Armani or blue jeans.

He gathered his keys and badge wallet and went out to the parking lot to his car. He drove to the precinct and found no space to park in the lot. Looked like they had brought everyone in today, he thought. He saw the federal vans for the task force parked up front. He wondered if anyone he knew from his days on the FBI team was there.

He managed to squeeze into a spot almost on the sidewalk. Too bad, he thought, people could walk on the grass. He exited his car and went in past the desk sergeant who waved to him. A couple officers commented about him being suspended.

"They need me here more than a suspension could stop me," he said back with a laugh, and proceeded to the squad room where there was a flurry of activity from the police and the feds.

Doyle entered the room and went around to the captain's office. The captain was in with two men in suits who reeked of FBI. Doyle could see the one agent, who he didn't know, but the other was behind a partition and Doyle couldn't make him out. He stood outside the office until the captain saw him and waved him in.

Doyle entered the room and the agents both turned to look him over. Doyle now knew the unidentified man. He had served with him on the terrorist task force, Kent Simmons.

"Well, Kent, they trusted you to handle this?" Doyle asked the man.

"I had to, they knew you couldn't handle it," Simmons replied.

"Okay, cut the friendly banter, we have a situation. Sit, Doyle," the captain barked.

Doyle bristled at being ordered to sit like he was a dog. The captain, a big, black, overweight man named Thelonius Cadeem, was a holdover from the last administration that was investigated for corruption and selling drugs from the evidence lockup. Cadeem somehow survived the investigation and was promoted to captain. There were much better men for the job, Doyle always felt, but Cadeem was a good old boy with the upper brass. So he got the job. It's not what you know, it's who you know.

Doyle sat next to Simmons and listened. "The nanny had the two children, both boys, five and seven years old, in the city park. They were walking along a sidewalk going to her car when a van pulled up and four men got out. This is all according to witnesses. The men grabbed the boys as the nanny fought, she was shot in the process. The van fled the scene and witnesses called 911 for help. No one remembers the van, other than the color, white. Most of the witnesses were women in the park with kids, they didn't want to get involved."

"Figures," Doyle muttered.

The captain eyeballed Doyle and then continued, "An hour later, the Mayor's office got a call from the kidnappers. They said the Mayor was marked for death along with his boys if he didn't cooperate. What that cooperation is, we don't know. The kidnappers said they'd call again and hung up. The Mayor isn't happy that he doesn't know what they want. The city is in bankruptcy, so it can't be money. Besides, the Mayor can't get city funds without approval from the city council. He's not rich, so that can't be it. We just have to wait and see."

"Could be a prisoner swap," Doyle said. "One of their people in exchange for the mayor's boys."

"I can't think of anyone we have in custody that would qualify for a swap. Everyone we have is a lowlife," the captain said. "There isn't much more to do until we hear from the Mayor and the kidnapers. So, go out and relax until we have something."

Doyle left the captain's office followed by the agents. Simmons took Doyle aside from the others to talk.

"Art, you left the bureau not a minute too soon. They started bringing down all kinds of new regulations and procedures for us. It was a mess. They brought in teams of psychologists to work with the profilers and completely changed everything. I think they watched too many TV cop shows about solving cases."

"Yeah, well, I'm not real happy here, either. Why did you stay?"

"I got myself transferred to investigations, the terrorist task force was getting to be too much. I heard you kicked the crap out of a perp last week. You're our hero of the week."

"Yeah, and I got suspended for it. I should have shot the guy and said he was trying to escape. It would have saved the city and me a lot of hassles."

"It's the most used excuse for all law enforcement. I've thought about it a few times. So what's the deal with Detroit?"

"Poor management and too many politicians screwing up. Our illustrious former mayor Kilpatrick is still stewing in jail. They want him to pay back millions. Good luck with that. I was hoping this new mayor would straighten out the city. Now we need to get this mess taken care of and put the family back together so he can concentrate on the city."

Captain Cadeem yelled across the room to Doyle. "The massa calls. I be a good slave and go see what the massa needs," Doyle mimicked to Simmons. They both chuckled. He left the man and went around the desks back to the captain's office. The captain was now at his desk, sitting back smirking as Doyle entered.

"Sit, Doyle," he said. Doyle bristled again and sat. "I didn't want you back here, but you lucked out. The commissioner said you came recommended by some high mucky-muck in the FBI. They wanted

you, I didn't. I don't like you, Doyle. You're a
Neanderthal and you're crude. You don't play well
with others and you're arrogant."

"Gee, Captain, you know me so well," Doyle
said sarcastically, when Cadeem finally took a breath
between words.

"Shut up, Doyle. If it weren't for these boys, I
would have argued to leave you out of this.
Unfortunately, I know you are a good cop. I know
you can get this job done. So, do it without being a
wise ass. You hear?"

"Are you done, Captain?"

"Yeah, get outta my sight."

Doyle stood, thinking about the boys more than
his desire to strangle Cadeem. The man's neck was
too fat to strangle, so it would have to be a gun shot.
One bullet to his fat head. Doyle went out of the
office, slamming the door, just short of breaking the
glass. He felt like going back and slamming it harder,
but he took a breath and went to where the feds were
camped out in the squad room.

He went to Simmons and said quietly. "When
this case is over, I'm out of here."

"I'm sure you could come back to us. Come over
to the dark side and be a good little feebie. Special
Agent in Charge Warwick loved you. He'd be more
than happy to have you back."

"I'll keep it in mind. If I'm not in prison for
murdering Cadeem."

*

Chapter 3

The tension was high in the squad room as they waited on the kidnappers to call with their demands. Doyle sat with the FBI agents talking about his adventures in days past with the FBI. The noise level in the room was getting to be louder than Doyle liked, he thought about going outside for a break. He stood and told the men he was getting some air just as Cadeem's door flew open and he came charging out.

"I got the mayor's office on the phone, they want to talk to…" he paused and looked annoyed, "Geezus, they want to talk to Doyle."

Doyle was surprised at the request and didn't move. Why did they ask for him specifically? What was he to the kidnappers, or the mayor for that matter?

"Get your ass moving, Doyle, the mayor's office wants to talk you for some God-awful reason," Cadeem bellowed and went back in his office.

Doyle was still struck by the request and moved quickly to take the call. He entered the office and saw the phone handset on the desk. Cadeem pointed to it and scowled. "Take it," he barked.

Doyle picked up the phone and answered, "This is Detective Doyle."

He heard a cough and then a man said, "Doyle, you need to get to the mayor's office ASAP. Move now, don't delay."

"Who is this?" Doyle asked.

"Deputy Mayor Barnes. I was told to find you and get you here. Move now, Doyle, minutes count in the life of the mayor." He hung up.

Doyle stood with the phone, shocked, and then slammed it down. He turned and left the office quickly. Cadeem yelled, "Where you going, Doyle?"

Doyle stopped and turned, "I got an invite to the mayor's office." Doyle looked over to Simmons and gave him a nod that said to follow. Simmons got up and went out of the room after Doyle, who was already heading for the parking lot.

Doyle went to his Charger and opened the doors. Simmons jumped in and asked, "What up?"

"Don't know. I was told to get to the mayor's office, now," he said as he started the car. He backed out and headed out on the street towards the city hall. Doyle turned on the flashers and siren he had installed in his car and moved fast.

"It was the Deputy Mayor who I talked to and he said to go to the mayor's office. I haven't the faintest idea why I'm being called," Doyle spoke over the roar of his high performance engine.

"They know what a great cop you are and can handle this alone," Simmons said.

"I'm not the Lone Ranger," Doyle said with a smile as he maneuvered around the traffic on Woodward Avenue heading to Larned Street up to the Coleman Young Municipal Center, home of the mayor's office.

"Well, I'm not Tonto, either. You did something that brought attention to you."

"I'm usually getting into trouble. Maybe they want a rogue cop to handle this, so they called for the best rogue cop in the city," Doyle said with a smirk.

They arrived at the building and Doyle pulled into the police parking area in front. He threw the sign on his dash saying 'Police Business' and they went into the building. He had been by the mayor's office before, so he knew where to go. They had to bypass the security check point to scan for weapons with their metal detector grid. Doyle flashed his badge, as did Simmons, and the deputies waved them through.

They arrived at the office and the secretary told Doyle to go in. Simmons followed, but stayed back. There were about ten men in the office, all talking. They silenced when Doyle entered. Doyle looked around and didn't see the mayor. The deputy mayor came around the big desk to Doyle. "Good that you got here quickly. We don't have a lot of time. Please sit." He pointed to a chair in front of the desk and sat back in the mayor's chair. Doyle was amazed by what was happening.

"Here's the facts, in a nutshell. The mayor has been taken. He was told forty-five minutes ago to go to the parking structure, alone, or his boys would die. He thought maybe they were going to give the children back. He was naïve to think they would. The mayor demanded that all law enforcement stay away.

19

Doyle's Law

Our court officers weren't able to stop the men from taking the mayor. But, the good news is they dropped off the boys. They're with their mother in the other room. But, now they have the mayor. About ten minutes after the switch, the kidnappers called and demanded that you be here to receive a call from them in…" He looked at his watch and said, "in ten minutes. Just in time, Doyle."

"Why me, did they say?"

"No, they demanded that you be here. I'd like to know what your connection is to these men?"

"How the hell should I know? I'm just as surprised as you are. Have they identified themselves?"

"No, nothing about who they are. The facts at this time are very minimal. Everything is happening too fast."

A phone rang out in the reception room, the secretary answered. Then she yelled, "Kidnappers on line one."

Deputy Mayor Barnes pressed the speaker button on the desk phone and said, "Deputy Mayor Barnes."

The voice came through the phone speaker. "I don't want you, fool. Put Doyle on."

Doyle leaned to the desk, adjusting the chair to be more comfortable. "I'm right here, fool. What do you want?"

"Listen closely, Doyle, you put Marcus Howard in the hospital. Not a nice thing. We are not happy with you putting our homeboy in harm when we were looking for him. He weren't doing nothing bad, but disciplining a stupid girlfriend who was cheating.

You stuck your nose in this. We want Marcus back and you are going to bring him to us."

"And, you'll give me the mayor back, right? What's to say we won't come after Marcus after the exchange is made? I don't see you turning over the mayor that easily. You got more on your mind than one useless scumbag. Let's put the deal on the table."

There was a pause, they could hear muffled talking away from the phone. "You don't need to worry about Marcus, we are going to take good care of him. We just want him back for something he has. We don't want this idiot mayor, but you do."

"You know, if this goes down, every cop in the city will be looking for your sorry asses. Oh sorry, it's already too late for that, you already screwed up by taking the mayor. Why don't I trust you to make an exchange, the mayor for Marcus?"

Another pause, and more muffled talk. "I said we got no use for this fool. You want him back, we don't want him. We make the exchange, fair and simple."

"You could have just waited until Marcus's lawyers got him off and released. Why the hurry?" Doyle asked, figuring there was more to Marcus than they were letting on.

"We got little time to get something from Marcus. Time is of the essence, as they say. Both for you and us. You got until nine tomorrow morning to bring Marcus to us next to Cobo Hall Arena on Atwater Street by that big boat dock. Come alone or the mayor may lose his head."

"You do know Marcus is bandaged up pretty good. I'd have to bring him on a gurney."

"Slap him in a wheelchair, we don't care if he's in bad shape, as long as he can talk. Just be there. Alone." The phone clicked off, they hung up.

The police commissioner was in the room and said, "I can have snipers on top the Cobo Hall rotunda. It overlooks the boat docks."

"It may help if you want the mayor back. I'm sure these men will check everywhere before they put themselves out for attack," Doyle said. "I think Marcus has something they want and they want him back. The mayor is their leverage. I'll need an EMS unit to transport Marcus in his condition. You can put two of your best officers in as med techs. That's all I'll need on the ground."

"Pretty sure of yourself, Doyle. Think you can handle the situation?" Barnes said as he stood behind the desk.

"I'm never sure of anything until it happens. I usually have good luck in that way. I have no idea how many of them there are. Just reports that four men took the boys originally. So, we know there's at least four. If it's a gang, there could be more and they'd show up in force. I'd have no options then."

"Well, we have until tomorrow morning to form a plan," the commissioner said.

"You do what you have to do, I'm just the delivery boy. Just make sure your snipers don't shoot me. I have to go get Marcus ready for this." Doyle stood and headed to the door. "I'll be back."

Simmons followed Doyle out. "You're going to play rogue cop, aren't you?"

Doyle smiled and said, "I'm such a bad boy."

Chapter 4

They were in the car heading back to the precinct when Simmon's cell phone rang, he answered, listened, then hung up. "Well, bad boy, you're on your own. I've been called back to Lansing to do some actual investigating. Drop me off at my car and we'll kiss goodbye."

"You try and kiss me and I'll deck you. I want to go talk to Marcus at the hospital and see what his side of the story is. I'm surprised that his gang just didn't go into the hospital and take him out."

"Isn't he under guard?"

"I would imagine. Kind of dumb to have him as a prisoner and not have a guard on his room. Besides, we're not telling where he is."

"Well, I hope you figure out what it is they want from Marcus. I'm sure you'll foul up their plans. Just don't get the mayor killed. You won't be too well liked in Detroit."

"May be the time to get out of the city and go back north," Doyle said.

"You were from that area, weren't you?"

"Yep, I was born and raised in Oxford, just north of Lake Orion. My family lived there until they passed away. I sold the family home and bought a cabin out in Metamora, where I lived until I joined the FBI in Lansing. I kept the cabin, still go there when I need to refresh. I may end up there one day soon."

"Got a girlfriend?"

"Now you're getting personal. First a kiss, now asking about my love life. I wonder about you." Doyle smiled. "Yes, I sort of have a girlfriend. We live far apart, the best way to have a relationship. She's a lawyer and I don't like lawyers. But, I try not to think of her as a lawyer. She knows my feelings and tries to not talk about it. She works in Auburn Hills, far enough away, but still close."

"Any woman who can put up with you has to be a lawyer. Just to defend herself."

They arrived back at the precinct and Doyle parked. Simmons said to be careful and went to his car. Doyle didn't want to be seen by Cadeem, he would chew his ear off. Doyle went through the door and to the desk sergeant.

"Harold, I need you to do me a big favor. Call Oscar Drew and let me talk to him."

Harold smiled and dialed the number, waited and said, "Hold on please." He handed the phone to Doyle.

"Oscar, Doyle here. What's going on in the squad room?"

"A lot of unhappy people all waiting around for something on the kidnapping. Cadeem has been pacing around cursing you up and down. Not good for you to come in here."

"No problem. Can you pull up the file on Marcus Howard and find out what hospital he's in?"

"You going over to shoot him?" Howard asked as he punched up on the computer.

"Not until I get some facts from him."

"What's up with the kidnappers?" he asked, waiting for the computer to respond.

"Since you're doing me a favor, I'll share with you. They released the kids, but now they've got the mayor. Wait until I'm gone before you spread that," he laughed.

"Okay, he's at Henry Ford up by the Lodge freeway and West Grand Boulevard. No room number, just flash that smile at a nurse and they'll take you there."

"Thanks Oscar. I'll talk later if I don't get fired." He handed the phone back to Harold and thanked him.

He drove over to Henry Ford Hospital and parked in the front area for authorized vehicles. He put the sign back in the window and went in. The place was a tangle of people running around or dying on gurneys. He went to the desk and showed his badge.

"Hi, I'm looking for a prisoner who was brought in the day before yesterday. Marcus Howard," he asked the nurse.

She tapped some keys on her computer and said, "I have a Howard in restricted access. I presume that would be him." She told him where to go and he thanked her. He went to an elevator and waited. The door finally opened and a dozen people got out. He waited, then entered the car, pushing the button for the fourth floor. He watched the floor numbers flipping as the car rose. The thing stopped and he got off. He saw a cop he recognized sitting by a door and figured he found the right room.

The cop stood and said, "Detective, are you supposed to be here? I heard you were on suspension."

"They can't function without me. Thanks, Lyle. Is he awake?"

"Don't know, he's been real quiet. Just lying there every time I check in. You need to talk to him?"

"Just a couple questions. Lyle, if you hear any loud screaming, just ignore it please."

Lyle grinned and said, "What noise? I don't hear too well."

"Thanks Lyle." Doyle went into the room and found Marcus spread out on the bed, relaxing.

Doyle went up to the bed as Marcus turned his head and saw Doyle. His eyes got big, he turned and got a look of terror on his face. "You can't be in here," he recoiled.

"Marcus, Marcus, I just need to ask you a few questions," Doyle said as he came to the bedside and leaned over to the man. Marcus slid down in the covers, but Doyle pulled the covers off of him, exposing the man.

"I'll call for help," he cried.

"Marcus, I just need to talk to you. You're a popular man. Your gang is wanting to get their hands on you."

That made Marcus cringe further. "Marcus, you look frightened. Is there a reason you should be frightened?"

"Don't know what you're talking about," he replied.

"Well, your friends kidnapped the mayor of Detroit and they want to trade him for you. So, you must be an important man."

"The mayor? They took the mayor for me?"

"Yes, and I'm supposed to swap you in the morning for the mayor. You have a short life span, I would say." Doyle could see the terror in his eyes. "Marcus, talk to me. Tell me what your homies want and maybe I can help you. What is it that they want?"

"I don't know what you're talking about," Marcus said defiantly and pulled the pillow over his head.

Doyle grabbed the pillow and pushed hard on his face. He was now struggling to break free. His arms were flailing and grabbing at Doyle's arms.

Doyle finally pulled the pillow away and flung it across the room. "Now, do you want to talk? Your life is in my hands."

"I still don't know what you want," he moaned.

Doyle grabbed his bandaged arm and squeezed. Marcus screamed in pain. "Okay, what do you want?"

"Tell me what your friends want from you? Why are they going to all this trouble to get you back?"

Marcus went quiet as Doyle backed away. He had tears in his eyes now. Doyle didn't feel sorry for the man.

"I took a huge shipment of drugs from them. They want them back."

"Where are the drugs, Marcus?"

"That's the problem, I don't know. My bitch of a girlfriend took them and hid them. I was trying to get the location from her when you stopped me from beating it out of her. I don't have them. Ask her."

Doyle wasn't happy. Now he had to find the girlfriend. "Where can I find her?"

"Hell, I don't know. Didn't you arrest her?"

"She was the victim, so they didn't take her in, other than for questioning. She refused to press charges, so we are holding you for attacking me. Where does she usually hang out?"

"She strips a couple nights a week at the Crazy Horse on Michigan. Otherwise, she sponges off different men."

"Sponges? She's a hooker? What's her name?"

"Twinkle Brightly," he replied.

"Come on, Marcus, do better than a nickname."

He was quiet then said, "Loretta Walsh. She lives around Bagley and Vermont. You can look her up in your database, she's been arrested before."

"Marcus, I'm supposed to trade you for the mayor in the morning. If I can find Twinkle, I can see if I can help you."

"Why would you want to help me, you beat the hell out of me."

"I don't like uneven numbers. Your gang gives you no chance to live. I'll even the odds. Who's the leader of your gang?"

"Crazy Joe Gold. He's the boss of the people who distribute drugs in the city. You get him and his people and you cut off a big chunk of drug dealings."

"Why did you take the drug shipment?"

"Money, of course. Are you stupid?"

"I may be, but you're the one in trouble. Thank you, Marcus, I'll be back."

Doyle went to the door and out. The cop stood and said, "Is he still alive?"

"Yep, unfortunately. I'll need him alive in the morning. Don't let anyone get near him, unless you are sure they belong there. Thanks, Lyle."

Doyle left the hospital and made a call. "Oscar, how's things in the precinct?"

"Mad. There is a big hoo-ha around here over the mayor being taken. The commissioner has ordered everyone to stand down except a few people he wants to spearhead the attack on the perps. The feds aren't happy, but a call from the commissioner to the FBI headquarters has issued a pull back of the agents. Cadeem is steaming about you being away."

"Good, I hope he has a heart attack. I need you to look up one more name, a woman."

"Looking for a date?" he laughed.

"No, she's a stripper. I can get my own dates."

*

Chapter 5

Doyle gave the name, Loretta Walsh, and waited while Oscar tapped away at the keyboard. Doyle was standing by his car and watched as a couple ambulances roared in to the ER entrance. Orderlies and nurses rushed out to bring the gurneys in. There were four gurneys altogether, Doyle figured it was a gang fight or a pile up of cars on the freeway. Oscar was humming to himself as he was still typing.

"I thought computers were fast? What's taking so long?" Doyle asked.

"I got to check different databases. This isn't like on TV where the name pops up the first try. Is this Loretta aka Twinkle Brightly?"

"Yeah, that's the one. You got an address?"

"1312 Bagley, apartment four. Going for some entertainment?"

"What I need to know won't be entertaining. Thanks, Oscar. You haven't heard from me."

"Who are you again?" Oscar laughed and hung up.

Doyle got in his car and drove out from the hospital. On his way to Loretta's, his cell phone played *Jaws* again and he looked at the caller ID. It was Cadeem. He pushed the button to ignore the call and put the phone back in his pocket.

"Screw you, Cadeem. I've had enough of your crap." He thought more about getting out of the job. Maybe retire to his cabin and live off the land. He wasn't crazy about gardening, but he could hire some local kids to come in and set up a garden for him. Maybe have some chickens and a couple cows for milk and hamburgers. That's the ticket, Farmer Doyle. He laughed out loud at the thought.

He was cruising down Bagley, looking for Loretta's address. This part of the neighborhood wasn't bad, mostly middle class families. He wondered how Twinkle Brightly fit in with the Joneses. He found the address, it was an old apartment building probably built in the thirties. It was kept up well and there were bicycles out front. Great, children and strippers in one housing area.

He parked the car out front. There weren't a lot of cars on the street so he had no problems. He got out and went to the stoop of the building. The old metal push button panel with the tenants' names was well worn. Some of the buttons had no name associated with them. He knew she was in apartment four, but didn't want to spook her into running, if she was even in the building. He found the button for the building manager and pressed it.

A voice came through the speaker box and said, "What ya want?"

Doyle looked around for cameras, but saw none. "Building inspector, I need to see your basement," he said, hoping the manager wasn't a hard ass.

"Geezus, you guys just checked it last month. Hold on." He clicked off and Doyle waited. About two minutes later, a fat man in a robe trudged up stairs that could be seen through the glass in the front door.

He walked up to the door and looked at Doyle through the glass. Doyle held his badge to the glass so the manager could see it. He frowned and unlocked the door.

"You ain't no building inspector."

"No, he just left. But, I'm here to see one of your tenants. Apartment four."

"You wanna to see the ho? Are you buying or arresting?"

"Questioning. Now may I come in?"

"I ain't gonna stop you. I wish you'd get her outta here. She lowers the value of the property."

"I'll see what I can do. Thanks." Doyle went through the door when the fat man moved away. He pointed to stairs going up and told Doyle she was up there. Doyle climbed the stairs and finally got to the second floor before finding apartment four. He saw there were two apartments for each floor and went to the door.

He knocked gently on the door and waited.

"Who that?" came a female voice from the other side.

"Room service," Doyle responded.

"We ain't got no room service. Don't screw with me," she yelled back.

"Crazy Joe sent me about Marcus."

It got really quiet. Then Doyle heard what sounded like a window being opened. He brought up his foot and kicked in the door. Loretta, he presumed,

32

was trying to lift the window, but it wasn't going up all the way. She screamed as Doyle came toward her, then she stopped.

"You is a cop. You didn't come from Crazy Joe or Marcus. Whatcha want cop? I ain't done nothing wrong," she said, looking to feel a bit more relaxed.

"I did come from seeing Marcus… in the hospital. He told me an interesting story about a missing shipment of drugs. He tells me you know something about its whereabouts."

"I don't know from no whereabouts of any drugs. Marcus is a jive ass bitch." The woman was standing with her back to the wall, looking defiant. Suddenly, she changed her expression. "Hey, you that cop who beat up Marcus in the alley. You shaking us down for something?"

"Loretta, I only want to know where the drugs are and save your life."

"What ya mean, save my life? From who?"

"Crazy Joe, once he finds out you have the drugs."

"Who's gonna tell him? You?"

"No, Marcus. Once I turn him over to Crazy Joe in the morning."

"Why you wanna do something like that? That be crazy," she said.

"Well, it seems Crazy Joe is holding the Mayor of Detroit hostage and wants to trade him for Marcus. We have no choice but to swap. Once Joe has Marcus, he'll know you have the drugs."

"Joe won't believe Marcus. He's a lying son-of-a-bitch."

"Don't matter. Joe will wonder if you do and come looking for you. If you give me the drugs I can keep Marcus and you away from Joe. Unless you have a death wish."

"I ain't got no death wish. The only death I want to see is Joe's. He be a crazy bitch."

"Guess that's where he got his nickname. Now, you want to tell me where the drugs are?"

She didn't say anything. Doyle was watching her face and saw she glanced to a hallway quickly then looked away. Doyle went to her, grabbed her arm, and pulled her to the hallway.

"Hey, what the hell. Let go of my arm," she screamed as Doyle dragged her into the hallway. There were two doors, one open and one closed. The one opened was a bedroom. It was a mess. Bed sheets on the floor, clothes scattered around. Doyle looked at her and said, "Are the drugs in here?"

Her eyes involuntarily glanced to the closed door.

"Ah, you don't have much of a poker face." He pulled her to the closed door and opened it. Doyle just had enough time to see the shotgun aimed at him before he dropped to the floor and pulled his Sig. He blasted the gunman a second before the shotgun fired, barely missing Loretta. The gunman collapsed to the floor dropping the shotgun in front of Doyle. He reached out and pulled the shotgun away, cracking it open to remove the unused shells.

"Any more surprises?" he said to the woman also on the floor. She said nothing. "Crap, now someone will call the cops and we'll be overrun with them."

"Ain't nobody calling the cops. These people are used to gunfire," she said as she stood.

Doyle got up from the floor and looked around the room. On the bed he saw a large suitcase, the kind used to haul things other than clothes. He grabbed Loretta and pulled her in the room. She tripped over the body of the man bleeding out on the floor rug and went down.

"Damn, don't be so rough," she wailed.

Doyle opened the suitcase and found bags of what looked like cocaine. Lots of it. "Well, this would be a tidy sum for whoever has it. I'm sure Crazy Joe would like it back."

Doyle pulled his cell phone and dialed Oscar again. "Hey, I need you to make a call to dispatch and send some cars to that address you gave me earlier. Got a body and a suitcase full of coke for pickup. Call Narco, too, and let them know about the coke. Loretta should be detained for questioning."

"Doyle, you just don't know how to stay out of trouble. The commissioner has been calling for you, too. You better get back with them. They're getting antsy about the swap tomorrow morning."

"Thanks, I need to go back to the hospital and check out our patient. I'm going to put him in a safe place. That's between you and me."

"Sounds like you may need some help. I'm about ready to go off shift."

Doyle thought about it. "Might be a good idea, what I have in mind may need some backup. You know where my apartment is, I'll meet you there." They hung up and Doyle went to Loretta. He pulled a plastic flexi-cuff out of his jacket and pulled her to the radiator. He strapped her wrist to it while she complained and protested.

"You'll be fine once the police get here. Don't struggle, that band can cut your wrist." He stood and wondered if she'd chew her hand off to escape. He laughed at the thought and looked around, then went downstairs to the front door. The manager was standing by the door as Doyle approached him.

"The police are on the way. I would suggest you stay away from the apartment."

"Is she leaving?"

"She will be, for a long time." Doyle smiled and went out to his car.

*

Chapter 6

Doyle cruised over to his apartment and pulled in the parking lot. He saw Oscar sitting in his beat up Chevy Impala. Doyle honked and Oscar got out of his car and went to Doyle. He got in and said, "So, I'm about eight months from retiring. Am I going to get fired for this?"

"I'll be right beside you for unemployment. Thanks for offering to help. I don't have a lot of time to make this up and hope it works."

"You do have a plan?"

"Actually, I'm going with plan B. Plan A sucked. We need to get Marcus out of the hospital and put him in my apartment. Then I'll need to talk to the commissioner about transportation in the morning. We have work to do tonight to get ready."

"Yep, we are going to get fired," Oscar said.

Doyle drove back to Henry Ford and parked in front again. He and Oscar went in and to the elevator. On the way up, Doyle said, "Lyle Talbot was on duty, the last I saw, so he shouldn't be a problem. I may need him to help, too. A cop in uniform shows that we know what we're doing."

"Now Lyle is going to get fired. We may as well start a club," Oscar said.

"Knock it off, Oscar," Doyle said as the doors opened to the floor. They got out and went to the room. Lyle was still on duty and smiled as the men approached.

"Boy, Marcus has been a bear about your visit. The nurses weren't too happy either," Lyle said.

"Well, the nurses are going to be less than happy over what I'm going to do. I'll need your help, too. Grab that wheelchair and follow us," Doyle instructed, pointing to a chair down the hall.

"Oh, man. Are you back again?" Marcus moaned, when the men came in the room. "Brought some help this time to work me over, right?"

"Marcus, shut up. We want to keep you alive. Unless you'd rather take your chances with Crazy Joe?" Doyle went to Marcus and started pulling wires off him from the machines that monitored his progress. "Hey, that stuff is keeping me alive, don't do that."

"Let me know if you start dying," Doyle said as he pulled the man up and slid his legs over the side of the bed.

"Lyle, bring the chair here." Lyle brought the chair up next to the bed and set the wheels. Doyle and Oscar lifted the man to the chair, Marcus started complaining again. "You keep that up and I'll give you something to hurt about," Doyle threatened him.

Doyle grabbed a blanket and covered Marcus' legs, then he told Lyle to get the door. The men wheeled Marcus out in the hallway. Doyle whispered to him, "If you want to live, keep your mouth shut, or I swear to God, I'll shoot you."

Marcus nodded his head quietly. Two nurses came out from the nurses' station on the other side of the elevators and saw the small parade of men.

"Just what are you doing taking this man? He hasn't been released or checked by a doctor yet," a big nurse said.

"Move, Nurse," Doyle yelled, showing his badge. "We have to get this man into protective custody, ASAP. There are men coming for him with guns, and they could be here any minute. I would suggest you go back to your station and call security to come and protect you. Do it now!" he said in a loud authoritative voice.

The nurse looked confused, then turned and ran back to the station, followed by the second nurse.

"We need to move fast, now," Doyle said as he was punching the button outside the elevator.

"You know you aren't racking up points with the hospital," Oscar said.

"Yeah, yeah. I'll try not to get shot and be brought here." Doyle pushed the wheelchair into the car when the door opened.

They waited as the car descended to the ground floor. They rushed through the confusion of the lobby and out to Doyle's car.

"Put him in the back seat," Doyle said as he opened the door and pulled the seat forward. Marcus wasn't happy about being pushed around and said so.

"Man, I didn't ask for this treatment," he moaned.

"Yes, you did. When you became a criminal. Now, shut up and sit back." Doyle turned to Lyle and said, "Thanks, man. Help Oscar put the chair in the trunk and then get lost. Go back to your station and if they ask, tell them I relieved you."

"Good luck, I hope it works out for you," Lyle said and wheeled the chair back to the trunk.

"I hope it works, too," Doyle muttered.

"What did you say?" Oscar asked, standing by the trunk.

"I said it will work. It's plan B."

"Why don't I believe you?" Oscar said with a frown.

"Just get in the car and let's get out of here."

Doyle's Law

Doyle drove out and back to his apartment. He pulled around to the back of the building so they wouldn't be seen hauling a bandaged patient into the building. Doyle popped the trunk and Oscar helped him to remove the wheelchair. They brought it around and opened the door, pulling Marcus out and into the chair. He didn't say a word this time, which pleased Doyle. Oscar closed the door and the trunk as Doyle pushed Marcus to the building. He turned the chair around and pulled it up the short steps to the back entrance. Oscar held the door while Doyle pulled the chair in.

"I'm glad you're on the first floor. I'm not wanting to haul his sorry ass up any stairs," Oscar said.

"I should make him walk in, but I did break his leg. I'll remember that next time I beat up a perp. Just in case he has to walk," Doyle said as he handed the keys to Oscar to open his apartment door. They entered and Doyle pushed Marcus to the center of the main room.

"Love your decorating. Early ghetto," Oscar said.

"If you don't like it, ignore it. What you see is all me."

Marcus said, "I've seen better flop houses."

"Did anyone pull your chain? If I want your opinion, I'll ask. Now just sit there and be quiet. We need to go over plan B," Doyle said.

"You actually have a plan B? And, why am I afraid to find out what it is?" Oscar asked.

"You'll love it, you get to play Marcus," Doyle replied.

"I knew I wasn't going to…what! What exactly do you mean I'm going to play Marcus? I'm not black or injured. How am I going to get away with that?"

"You'll see, and you'll love the simplicity of my plan. First, I have to call the commissioner to set up transportation."

Doyle left the men and went to a phone in the kitchen. He didn't use his cell phone so his number wouldn't be listed anywhere. Cadeem had it, but he was all who did. He checked his contacts and found city hall again and dialed. A pleasant female voice answered. "Detroit City Hall, may I help you?"

"Yes, this is Detective Art Doyle, I need to be connected to the Police Commissioner's office."

"One moment, please." She put him on hold and he listened to some really bad muzak. About two minutes later, another pleasant female voice came on. "Commissioner Jenkens office. How may I help you?"

"Detective Doyle here, I need to talk to the commissioner."

"Yes, Detective, he has been trying to reach you. I'll put you through." She clicked off and Doyle waited again.

"Doyle, where the hell have you been? I got everyone trying to organize this attack and you're missing," came the man's voice.

"Yes, sir, I've been working on my plan to free the mayor."

"Your plan? I got tactical officers here who are preparing this, what makes you think you can plan it?"

"Because I'm the one they want to deliver Marcus. Who, by the way is missing. I know where he is and I'm taking him to the drop point in the morning. Now, I need a couple things and I can get on with this."

There was silence on the other end for far too long. Had he pushed the boss too hard? Oh well, he figured, he wanted to get off the police force - what better way than to aggravate the commissioner of police? Finally, he heard breathing.

"I'm not happy, Doyle. But, I know your reputation for being a cowboy, and from what I hear, you do get the job done. I'll excuse your insubordination and let you handle this. We're going to have backup and snipers ready in case this goes bad. So, be aware. What is it you want?"

"I need an EMS unit, with two medically trained cops in those clothes med techs wear. I'll explain to them what I need in the morning. Have them meet me in the parking lot on 3rd Street and Fort Street at seven o'clock. We have some preparation to do."

"Alright, but if this goes bad, it will be your ass," he said and hung up.

"Great way to pass the buck, you pompous jerk." Doyle hung up and went back to the others. "Okay, I got the commissioner on my side, so we are good to go."

"I'm still a little shaky on just how I'm going to became Marcus," Oscar asked.

"Well, sit down and I'll go over plan B. You'll love it."

*

Chapter 7

Doyle's apartment was small, so they had to make do with the limited sleeping options. Oscar had won a coin flip and was snoozing soundly in Doyle's bed. Marcus was assigned the couch, handcuffed to a decorative spindle on the wooden arm. Doyle slept on the recliner, it wasn't the first time. He'd been awake late thinking about the morning and what could happen. He often worried about what the day would bring. Would he get mad and shoot someone who pissed him off? Worse yet, would he get shot? He had been shot before, luckily nothing serious, but he remembered the pain the bullet caused as it tore into his flesh. He had been lucky so far not to get killed. When he finally nodded off, he slept fairly well.

Morning came and Doyle was up getting ready. Oscar was in the kitchen making something that smelled passible. Doyle wasn't a breakfast eater, it weighed heavy in his stomach. His first meal of the day was usually lunch at a local deli. Today he would have to pass up that lunch.

"I'm not happy with your plan, but it sounds plausible. I hope these hoods don't want me to talk. I don't do jive talk very well," Oscar said as he wolfed down what looked like eggs.

"This should all go down fast, so I don't think there will be time to talk. Just follow the plan and we should be alright."

"If I get shot, I'm shooting you," Oscar said, taking the last bite from the plate.

"I think we would both get shot. But, I hope not. Now, let's get moving."

"What about me?" Marcus said from the couch. "You didn't share your plan with me. Am I involved?"

Doyle handed him the TV remote. "Your job is to sit here and watch Oprah, or whoever is on."

"Oprah stopped doing her show. I can watch Wendy Williams, now."

"Good, you do that and be a good little hood."

Marcus gave Doyle a dirty look but said nothing. Doyle loaded his guns in their holsters and put on his jacket. He left the tie on the dresser - screw protocol. The gangsters aren't going to judge him on style.

"Let's go. We have to meet the EMS and get you ready." Doyle pushed the wheelchair to the door and they went out.

"You think he'll be here when we get back?" Oscar asked.

"Frankly, I hope he runs. As long as it isn't to where we're going."

They put the wheelchair in the trunk and Doyle drove out of the parking lot. He headed over to the parking lot where he had set up the meet. As he approached the lot, he saw an EMS unit along with two patrol cars. God, they just can't follow plans, he thought. He pulled up to the EMS unit and parked. He got out of the car and saw the men standing behind the vehicle. That's when he saw Cadeem.

Doyle's stomach turned sour, but he was prepared for Cadeem's bullshit. Doyle heard Oscar say a couple swear words under his breath as they went around the car to get the wheelchair from the trunk.

"About damn time you got here, Doyle," Cadeem yelled.

"I'm early, just as you are, Captain. I'm not late," Doyle said, gritting his teeth.

Oscar took charge of the chair and they went to the men.

"Who's the EMS officer?" Doyle asked.

One man held his hand up. "Good, we need to get this man ready. I'll explain."

"You better explain it to me before you do anything stupid, Doyle," Cadeem growled.

Doyle went nose to nose with the fat man. "Look, Captain, I got the okay from the commissioner to run this operation. If you have a problem with that, talk to him before you talk to me. Understand, Captain!"

Cadeem looked surprised. Doyle never talked back to him like that. He always had a smart remark, but was never outright hostile. He stood back and waited.

"Good. Now, I need Oscar to be bandaged up like a mummy. These perps don't know how badly I hurt Marcus, so we should be able to get away with it. Just one layer of gauze, so he can see well enough to do what we have planned. Give him two small eyeholes."

The officers who were going with Doyle sat Oscar down and started to work on him. Doyle went to his car and took a short barreled shotgun from it. He took it to Oscar and put it on the chair to Oscar's right.

"That all you got?" Oscar asked.

"You got your service piece, use it," Doyle said, referring to the .38 Chief's Special Smith and Wesson that Oscar favored.

The last bit of Oscar's face was wrapped. Doyle said it was an improvement. Cadeem was pacing, mumbling to himself. Doyle ignored the man.

"Okay, let's get him in the back of the unit." Doyle put a blanket over Oscar's legs, hiding the shotgun, then wheeled him to the opening and the men lifted him inside. Doyle explained what he wanted them to do and they agreed.

"We got fifteen minutes, may as well head over." Doyle climbed into the back while the two officers went to the cab. They drove out as Doyle watched though the window in the door, Cadeem stood with two other patrol officers. He didn't look happy. They went to their cars and Doyle hoped they would stay back and not screw up the plan.

They drove down 3rd Street over to West Congress and around Cobo Hall to the Civic Center

Drive. Doyle was looking out the front through the small opening that connected to the cab. He could see the big boat docked and then saw a white van. It had to be them.

Doyle told them where and how to park for their best advantage. He hoped these creeps were too stupid to figure out his plan. The officers posing as EMS techs parked where Doyle instructed them to. Doyle opened the back door and got out.

The van had two men in front; the passenger got out when he noticed the ambulance. The driver stayed in the van. Doyle told the two 'med techs" to get out and come back to get the chair.

Doyle heard the man by the van yell, "I told you to come alone."

"Screw you, I can't carry Marcus by myself. You want him, I brought him," Doyle replied.

They had Oscar out and facing the van. "What the hell did you do to him, Doyle? He looks like a friggin mummy."

"I get a little carried away sometimes."

"How do I know that's Marcus?" the man asked.

Doyle changed the subject quickly. "Are you Crazy Joe Gold? Where's the mayor? You got him or not? I need to see him." Doyle threw out the questions to divert attention from Oscar.

"Yeah, I'm Crazy Joe. And I'll show you how crazy I am if you're screwing with me." He went to the back of the white van and banged on it, the doors opened. Two men got out and pulled the mayor out with them. His hands were tied in front and he looked frazzled.

"Fine, you said alone, but I see you got your people with you."

"I don't trust cops, now give me Marcus."

"Send the mayor over first," Doyle demanded.

"No deal. Send Marcus."

Doyle went behind the wheelchair and took the handles. Oscar whispered, "This better work."

"Shut up, unless you can sound black." Doyle pushed the chair halfway across the parking lot then gave the chair a good push. It rolled over to the two men at the back of the van. So far so good, Doyle thought. Doyle walked towards the front of the van where Crazy Joe and the mayor were.

"Now, send me the mayor, and no tricks," Doyle said. He glanced at Oscar as one of the men were leaning to him.

"Hey, Joe, this guy is too big to be Marcus," the man yelled.

"What?" Joe yelled back just as Oscar brought out the shotgun and blasted the man's midsection. He went down and then Oscar shot the other man.

Joe grabbed the mayor and used him as a shield as Doyle brought out his Sig Sauer.

"Damn you, Doyle, just couldn't do this easily, could you? I'll kill this bastard unless you get everyone out of here." Doyle saw the driver get out and noticed the automatic weapon in his hand. Doyle took aim, eased on his trigger, and took the man down with one shot.

The two men in the EMS unit came running out dressed in flax vests and carrying assault rifles. They stopped, one on each side of Doyle.

"Looks like you're alone now, Joe. You can go out in the ambulance, or you can surrender."

"Screw you, Doyle, I got the mayor, you'll listen to me," Joe said as he cocked the gun in his hand and aimed at the mayor's head.

Doyle moved closer to the two men - Joe had nowhere to go, his back was to the van. Doyle took a calculated risk and aimed for Joe's head.

"No, Screw you, Joe." Doyle took the shot and Joe's head snapped back, the bullet impacting his head. Unfortunately, the bullet grazed the side of the mayor's head also, and a small stream of blood began to run down his face.

Joe dropped to the ground in a heap. The mayor was looking totally shocked, felt his wound and started screaming, "Geezus H. Christ. You shot me. What the hell were you doing? You could have killed me. I can't believe you did that. I'll see you are pulled from your job and when I'm through with you, you won't even be able to get a job as a security guard." The mayor was covering his wound and getting blood on his shirt.

The two officers acting as EMS techs hurried to the mayor and guided him to the unit. On the way, the mayor was screaming various swear words as Doyle stood there in a daze.

Oscar approached him and said, "Ungrateful asshole. You save his butt and he's upset over a graze. So, he'll have a nice scar to brag about his adventure, at least he's alive."

Doyle was silent. He was listening to the mayor still bitching and screaming from whatever the officers were doing to him. He could see more cop cars streaming down the road to the parking lot.

"It's going to get busy soon. I don't need this crap," Doyle said and smiled at Oscar. "I need a ride out of here. You should be alright. You didn't shoot the asshole. Take care, Oscar, I appreciate everything you've done for me." Doyle turned and walked to the road and to a patrol car that just pulled up. He said something to the officer getting out and both of them got in the car and drove off.

Oscar stood watching the car pull away, thinking, he's done for sure.

*

Chapter 8

One month later, Doyle stood on the porch of his cabin staring out at the water. He felt relieved not having to deal with criminals and the bureaucracy of the police state. The day after the incident, the papers told the tale of how the mayor was shot during a hostage situation. Of course, Doyle was mentioned as being the shooter. They didn't even make mention of how the mayor was saved by Doyle. He went into the precinct and into Cadeem's office. Cadeem immediately started yelling, Doyle reacted by pulling his service weapon, the .38 he'd grown so fond of, next to his Sig Sauer, and slammed it on Cadeem's desk, causing the fat man to jump. Then Doyle pulled his badge, threw it at Cadeem and said, "Here, shove this up your fat ass."

That was the last time Doyle was in the precinct. He heard that the mayor wanted him investigated. But, with his resignation, the investigation was moot.

Doyle smiled as he heard a car drive up the road and park out front.

He turned, anticipating seeing Gwen, but was surprised to see Oscar.

"What the hell you doing here?"

"Just wanted to see if you hung yourself in your cabin. I'm disappointed."

Doyle smiled and offered Oscar a seat. They sat on the old wooden lawn chairs that came with the cabin.

"How you holding up, Art?" Oscar asked.

He looked at his friend and said, "That's the first time you've called me by my first name."

"You know, it took me until last week to realize that your name is the same as the guy who created Sherlock Holmes. Arthur Conan Doyle."

"At least my parents didn't use Conan in my name. They did use John, which was Dr. Watson's first name. Arthur John Doyle is what I was stuck with. My dad loved Holmes. I became a cop, which pleased him immensely."

"Now you're becoming a private investigator. I would have expected you to get out of the business."

"How did you know?"

"You ran into Samuels last week and told him, he told me. Why a P.I.?"

"I enjoy investigating. Crime has become too open, an easy solve, every gangbanger and disgruntled spouse is murdering these days. The gangbangers want everyone to know they did it, and the spouses are too stupid to realize they are the first person we are going to investigate. I want a good mystery so I can use my great powers of deduction, like Holmes." He paused and then continued, "What are you doing now? Still with the 4-6?"

"I took an early retirement on full pension. They want us old farts to get out so they can bring in all those young punks who shoot first and then investigate." He paused, looking out to the water. "Nice view. Are you going to set up shop here in the country? I don't see a lot of call for a P.I. out here in the woods. Do the bears need your services?"

"There are a lot of thieving raccoons that need to be arrested," he laughed. "I'm going to set up in Detroit, more crime and less interference now from people like Cadeem. I still have the city apartment to live in and found a decent little store front to convert into an office."

"I hope the mayor doesn't find you."

"Let him, I'll graze the other side of his face to even him up." He sat thinking, "What are you going to do now?"

"I don't know. I've been a cop for over thirty years. I've got no other skills. My pension is barely enough to live on, but I can't party too hard."

"Feel like becoming a P.I.? I could use an extra hand."

Oscar sat quietly staring out at the water. "If I did, would my name be on the door?" he asked.

"Below mine, in smaller letters, sure."

"Okay, I'll go start the paperwork for my license. Have you got any cases yet?"

"Hey, I haven't even got the office set up. Let's take this a day at a time."

Doyle heard another car drive up. He and Oscar looked to the path to see who'd pop up. It was Gwen. Doyle stood and went to her, giving her a quick kiss. He brought her up the porch and to Oscar.

"Gwen, this is Oscar Drew, my partner in crime. Oscar, this is Gwen."

Oscar stood and took her hand, shaking it. "You poor woman," he said.

"Ignore him, he's a smart ass," Doyle said. "What brings you out here, besides me?"

She looked like she was trying to find words. She glanced at Oscar and then said to Doyle, "Can we talk?"

"Uh, oh. That doesn't sound good. Excuse us, Oscar." He took Gwen by the arm and led her into the cabin. He stopped and turned to her. "What's up?"

She turned away from him and looked out the window. He gave her the time to get it together. He felt something bad was coming. Nothing unusual in his life lately. She turned back to him.

"Art, my job at Rash and Hunt is going well. Too well. I've been asked to help open a new branch office."

"That's good, isn't it?"

"Well, the branch office is in Columbus, Ohio," she said.

"Oh. Well, that's a ways away, isn't it?"

"It is. I'm not sure if I could maintain a long distance relationship from there. It was bad enough here. I know you're starting over, you don't need to worry about having to keep me happy where I'm at."

"Well, we haven't had the greatest relationship. So, I guess it's time to call it a night and say goodbye," he sighed.

She went to him and hugged him. "I care about you, Art. But my life is getting complicated and I need to keep my head clear."

"No problem, as you said, I'm starting over. It's going to be a fresh start all around now with you gone."

"For both of us. I wanted to tell you in person, not by email or text."

"That's decent of you. Thanks."

She backed up and said, "Well, I'll be going. I have to leave tomorrow and I have so much to pack. Thank you, Art, you are a hell of a man."

She gave him a quick kiss on the cheek, walked around him and went out the door. He stood there as he heard her say goodbye to Oscar, and then a few minutes later, he heard the car start up and drive away. His emotions were mixed. He quit his job, was moving into a new one and just lost his girlfriend. He went back out and sat.

Oscar, said, "Should I ask?"

"She's moving out of the state. I'm really starting over. You're the only holdover from my past life. I don't know if that's good or not."

"Hanging yourself in your cabin is looking better right now, eh?"

Doyle gave Oscar the finger and laughed.

"It's getting late, feel like staying the night? We can have a bonfire and dance naked under the moon."

"You don't want to see me naked. But I'd like to stay, just to make sure you don't drink yourself into a stupor over lost love."

"It's not that bad, I was figuring we wouldn't last. She had her agenda, I had mine, and we weren't on the same path. Let's run into town and get more beer."

"That works for me." They got up and went to the car.

Around eleven o'clock, the men were watching the fire in the pit flaming up. "This isn't too bad," Oscar said. "I could get to like this."

"I'm not selling the cabin and I live alone. So find your own place."

They both continued to watch the fire and were silent.

The next morning, Oscar was in the area where the kitchen was set up. The cabin was one large room with one small bedroom and a bathroom. The kitchen was on one side of the room, and it had all the conveniences. Doyle had put in a microwave and a toaster. Oscar was waiting for Doyle to get up, he wasn't going to rush him. They both had a good amount of beer the night before to celebrate their new venture.

Oscar was sitting at the small kitchen table eating his food when Doyle staggered out. "Are you still here?" Doyle said.

"Did you want me to leave?"

He went to the table and sat. "No, I just thought you might have left me, too."

"Well, I'm not your girlfriend, so I'm still here. Besides, you hired me to work for you. I need the job."

"Well, we'll see how that goes. When my parents passed, I sold their house and bought this place. I had a good amount of money left over and put it away for a rainy day. Well, it's raining. I still have enough money to get set up and advertise the firm."

"What kind of advertising?"

"I thought about a TV commercial, like all those lawyers do."

"And annoy the viewers. I know you don't like lawyers, but they usually hire private investigators to do their leg work." Oscar said.

"Yeah I thought about that, too. We'll get some business cards printed and leave them with divorce attorneys for their cases. Nothing like following cheating spouses."

"What we need is one good murder case to solve and get our names in the papers. That will bring people in."

"Whatever, I'm going out for a morning swim," Doyle said and stood.

"Are you crazy, it's September and the temperature has to be in the low thirties."

Doyle looked at the thermometer outside the window. "Twenty-eight," he said. "It wakes me up."

"I can slap you a few times to wake you."

"Not the same. I'll be back in." Doyle went out the door in his robe and underwear and Oscar went to the window to watch. Doyle got to the water and stuck his foot in. He cringed and turned back to the cabin. He came back in and stood by the heater vent.

"If I ever start to do that again, just slap me hard."

*

Chapter 9

Doyle sat at the table and asked, "What happened after I left you at the boat dock that morning?"

"Well, I got interrogated for about an hour and a half as to what happened. The two cops in the EMS backed up my story. The brass wanted to know where you were, I told them you had another kidnapping to go to. They didn't find it funny. Cadeem was being his pompous self, complaining about how you shouldn't have been in charge. I was amazed that the whole thing went well, and took out the drug dealers. But the mayor was making such a fuss and everyone was trying to keep him happy. What a dipwad."

"I don't really care," Doyle said.

"I had a patrol car take me back to your apartment to get my car. Your car was gone so I figured you hit a bar to get drunk. What happened to Marcus?"

Doyle chuckled and said, "I went back to the apartment and found Marcus still on the couch watching TV. I uncuffed him and took him back to the hospital. He was complaining all the way about how he didn't like the service in the hospital. I was about ready to dump him on the side of the road." He smiled and then continued, "I got to Henry Ford and dropped him off at the front door and told him he was on his own. That was probably about the time you got to my apartment. I took the rest of the day off and drove around to contemplate my options. I decided to quit the force."

"I heard Cadeem wasn't happy when you came in his office and tossed your badge at him. I would have loved to have seen that."

"I'm glad never having to see his ugly face again. The next day, I went to the county building and got the papers to get my private license. It came in the mail last week. I ran around the city looking for a small, inexpensive office to work out of and found one on Michigan Avenue and Trumbull Street. Nice neighborhood and the rent isn't too bad."

"Hey, that's near where I live, how convenient," Oscar said.

"You got a wife?" Doyle asked.

"Divorced. Been that route three times. Hated every one of them. I was a fool for love, but an idiot for marriage. Luckily, they didn't want alimony. They knew how much I made as a cop and figured it wasn't worth it. How about you? Any wife in your past?"

Doyle was silent, Oscar gave him the space. "I had one wife. Married three years. She died in a car accident, drunk driver t-boned her. They said she went quickly."

"Sorry, Art," Oscar said sympathetically and they sat in silence.

"Well, life went on, and here we are talking like two old women about our lives. Get dressed and we'll go to the office and see what we need to do to get it ready to take on crime." Doyle stood and went to the bedroom.

An hour later they were heading down I-75 to Michigan Avenue and got off. Doyle drove to a row of buildings on the street and pulled into a parking lot in the back, followed by Oscar in his car. They got out and went around the front of the building and to one store front. Doyle took out some keys and opened the door.

"Wow, it looks like your apartment. Didn't the maid come in today?" Oscar said.

Doyle grabbed a broom leaning against a wall and handed it to Oscar. "The maid is now in the building."

Another two hours later, they had the place looking good, but it was empty. "We need some office furniture. Let's go over to the Salvation Army Thrift Store and see what they have." They locked up and went back to Doyle's car. Doyle knew where the thrift shop was and they arrived shortly thereafter.

"I love going through these places. Lots of old junk that I can buy to clutter my apartment," Oscar said.

"Remind me never to go to your apartment," Doyle said as he examined the desk and chair on the main floor. "This looks good, if we can get it delivered."

"I'm sure they'll bring it to you for a price."

Doyle inquired and they said they would deliver. Oscar found another desk and chair in the back of the room and yelled to Doyle. Doyle said to throw in the other desk set. They got a couple file cabinets that they put in the car, and drove back.

"Well, the file cabinets look nice," Oscar said, looking at them in the middle of the empty office.

"Give it time," Doyle said.

A week later, they had the place looking like an office. Furniture and potted plants to add to the ambience. Now they needed clients. Doyle had put an ad in the paper for a receptionist and told Oscar it would be his job to interview them.

"They don't need to be hotties, just a woman who can type, file and answer the phone."

"No hotties? That just isn't right. Mike Hammer had Velda, she was a hottie."

Bob Moats

"You're no Mike Hammer, either," Doyle said with a grin. "Just a good secretary with experience, please. And one who will work cheaply until we get rolling. I have to go to the printer and pick up our business cards. Hold down the fort." He left the building.

Oscar was wandering around the office admiring the look of it. The squad room he spent most of his life as a cop in was a dungeon compared to this. He felt good and hoped it was something that would lift Doyle's spirits. He seemed a little down hearted lately and not his usual self. Oscar wondered if losing Gwen may be catching up to him. He went and sat at his desk when the door opened and a woman came in.

She was plain looking, not beautiful, not ugly, Oscar thought. She was medium height and had very dark hair, almost too black. Maybe a dye job, he thought. Her clothing was thrift shop fashion, and she didn't look well off. She saw him and smiled.

"May I help you?" Oscar said, coming around his desk to her.

"I saw by the sign in your window that you are a private investigator?"

"Yes, we are. My partner is out, but should be back any minute," he answered, thinking this could be their first client. "Please, come and sit." He led her to the chair next to his desk and she sat. He went around the desk and sat, asking, "You are?"

"My name is Sara Kellogg. No relation to the cereal," she said with a smile. "I need help to find my father. He's gone missing, it's been three days."

"Have you been to the police?"

"No, I don't trust the police. My father has a record, and I don't want him to get in trouble if he's doing something he shouldn't. My father is a good man, but he gambles a lot and I fear he may have gotten in too deep with the bookies."

"You said he had a record. What were the charges?"

"Embezzlement from the bank he worked at. He stole money to gamble and he got caught. That was a couple years ago and he was finally released last month. But, he disappeared this week and I don't know where he's at. Can you help?"

"I'm sure we can do something. I'll need more info on your father to begin. Now understand, we just opened the business, so we are still getting organized, but we'll do what we can to find him. Where was the last you saw of him?"

"At home, he said he was going out to look for work. He never came back home that night. I didn't know what to do, I never knew his friends."

"Do you know any names of the bookies he may have used in the past?"

"I did hear him two weeks ago, talking to some man he called Louis, and he said he'd have money for him soon. I was afraid he got back into betting. I didn't confront him, maybe I should have."

"It hard to know what to do. Do you have a phone bill that I could see?"

"I just got one the other day, I can bring it to you."

"That may help. Drop it off later, if you could. Did your father have any favorite places to hang out, like a bar or place he would meet people?"

"I never knew where he hung out. If I had, I would have gone there."

"True. Give me as many details about your father as possible," he said and handed her a note pad and pencil. "Take your time filling it out. Everything you know about him, any small detail that might help."

She nodded and took the pad and started writing. Oscar sat back, watching her. He looked to the window out front and saw Doyle walking by, heading to the door.

"Excuse me, my partner is back." He stood and went to the door before Doyle entered. Doyle said, "I hope you're not going to welcome me every time I come in." Then he saw the woman. "Is she here for the job?"

"No, she's a client. Our first. Missing father with a gambling problem."

"How did she find us?"

"I didn't ask, but she said she saw the sign in the window."

"Glad I had that put up. You've talked to her?"

"I've got her giving us details about the man. Sounds like he got in too deep betting and he may be hiding out."

"Okay, from her clothing, she doesn't look like she can pay. I guess we will do this pro-bono to get the business started."

"My thoughts exactly," Oscar said.

Chapter 10

Oscar took Doyle over to the woman and introduced him. "Miss Kellogg, this is Art Doyle, the head P.I.," Oscar said jokingly. Doyle cracked a small smile. "Art, this is Sara Kellogg. No relation to the cereal company."

"How do you do? Oscar tells me your father is missing? How long?"

"Three days now. He left Monday morning to look for work and hasn't come back. I hope he's all right."

Oscar said to Doyle, "I'll fill you in on the details shortly."

"Well, we'll do our best to find him. We're a new firm and have a special going. First case is free."

The woman smiled and said, "Oh, that would be wonderful. I don't have much money, I was going to offer to pay in installments."

"Save your money, I like getting families back together," he said, thinking back to the mayor's kidnapped boys that started all this. "Oscar will take care of anything else we'll need from you to start our investigation."

"Thank you," she said and went back to writing. Doyle nodded to Oscar to follow him and went to his desk. He had two small boxes and opened one. They were business cards and Doyle pulled out one from the top box and handed it to Oscar.

"Hey, you got my name spelled right," he said.

"How hard is it to spell Oscar Drew?" Doyle replied.

"You'd be surprised how many times my first name has been mutilated. These are nice cards."

Doyle handed him the box and said, "Go take care of your client."

Oscar smiled and went back to Kellogg. She had finished writing and handed the pad back to Oscar. He looked it over and smiled.

"Very good, this should help us. Now, here's my card if you have any questions. But, please wait until we have something, we'll call you." He looked at the pad to be sure she left her number.

She stood. "Thank you so much. I didn't know who to turn to and I'm so worried about him. He goes to prison and I don't see him for years, then he comes home and goes missing. I feel so at a loss."

"Well, we'll do what we can to find him. If you could drop off that phone bill, it may help. Oh, and if you can bring a photo of him, it would help also." She opened her purse and took out a Polaroid photo of the man and handed it to Oscar. "Great, thank you."

Oscar followed her to the front door and held it open for her. She smiled and left.

"Did you take a picture?" Doyle asked.

"Picture? What picture? Of her father?"

"No, one of her, our first client, to put on the wall." Doyle gave him a big grin and sat at his desk.

Oscar laughed and said, "I'll take one when she comes back."

The front door opened again and in came a fairly attractive woman. She was in her early twenties, Doyle figured, and looked like she was trying to impress. She stood straight and presented herself formally as she held out her hand and said, "Mary Norman, I'm here about the job you advertised in the paper. I'm quite interested in working for a private investigating firm. If I qualify, that is."

Oscar was holding in a laugh at the young girl's attempt to look official. "Well, Miss Norman, shall we go talk?" He motioned her to his desk and she followed. Doyle got up and went to get the pad of paper from Oscar with the missing man's information. Oscar handed it to him along with the Polaroid photo. Doyle went back and sat down.

He studied the list of things that Leo Kellogg was into. He liked watching sports, drank moderately and was good at pool. Doyle tried to remember the last time he played pool, long ago. He looked at the photo of the man and saw a weary, well-aged person with grey hair and lots of wrinkles. He was sitting at what looked like a kitchen table with a bottle of beer in front of him. "A bottle man," Doyle said to himself, smiling. "A man after my own heart. Where are you Leo? Where have you gone to?"

The front door opened again and an older-aged woman in sensible dress came in. She looked like someone's grandmother and smiled at Doyle. He stood and went to her. "May I help you?"

She stuttered a little, probably from nervousness, and said, "I'd like to try out for the receptionist job. If you're still hiring."

"We're still interviewing, so if you'd have a seat, my partner will be with you shortly." He pointed to small couch sitting in front of the window looking out to Michigan Avenue. She walked over and sat primly. Doyle went back to the list. He saw that one of the things listed was that Leo was a Mason. He belonged to the Masonic Temple in Detroit. Doyle wondered if Leo's brother Masons excused his prison time. But, it was worth a check to see if any of his brethren had seen him lately.

Oscar tapped Doyle on the shoulder, breaking his concentration and annoying him that he was caught off-guard. "Art, do you want to talk to the first interviewee?"

"No, I'll trust your decision. You have another woman here for the job," he pointed to the grandma-type still sitting on the couch looking nervous.

"Thanks," Oscar said and went back to the young woman. He said something to her, she smiled and left the office. Oscar went to the older woman and introduced himself.

"Hello, I'm Oscar Drew, would you please follow me." He led her to his desk and asked her to sit, she did.

"And you are?" he asked.

"Marjorie Wayne, but you can call me Marge. I want to say right up front, that I haven't been employed for a number of years, but my husband passed about four months ago and I'm needing to get out of the house and do something." She paused and then said, "I'm sorry for rambling. But I'm nervous. As I said, I haven't worked for a while and I understand that times have changed. I see you had a young woman interviewing, you're probably looking for youth rather than an old woman like me. But I have experience."

"Marge, calm down. I'm not difficult to get along with. Now, what are your qualifications to be a receptionist?" Oscar sat back as the woman ran through a long list of jobs she had done in the past thirty years, since she was a young woman herself.

Doyle was listening to the conversation discreetly. He was getting a chuckle at the woman. She was a nice lady and, frankly, she was the kind of person Doyle would like to have working for them. The younger woman would eventually find a boyfriend, spend too much time partying with him, then get married and demand maternity leave to go have their twins. Too much hassle with younger women.

Marge finished and Oscar looked to Doyle to see if he had an opinion. Doyle nodded approval and Oscar said, "You sound great. We are a new firm and don't have a lot of funds to pay you."

She interrupted, "Oh, I'm not looking for a huge paycheck. I have nothing better to do at home. I'd even work for free to help you get started."

Oscar about fell back in his chair. Doyle stood and came over. "When can you start?" he asked.

"Any time you say," she replied.

"Okay, but this is going to be a trial run. We'll give you a week and then if you like us, and we like you, you'll have the job permanently."

"Agreed, I can start in the morning, if that's good."

"Yes, that will be fine," Doyle said. "Now, it will probably be quite boring for a while, so bring a book to read."

She laughed, "May I bring my knitting?"

"Only if you knit us scarves," Oscar spoke up.

"You tell me the colors and I'll do it."

"Fine, we'll see you first thing in the morning around eight," Oscar said, standing.

She beamed and said, "You have made an old woman very happy. Oh, and I have a .357 magnum, shall I bring it, just in case?"

Doyle looked surprised and asked, "Why do you have a gun?"

"My late husband was a policeman and he insisted I had a gun while he was out working. For protection. He even took me to the range to be sure I could handle it. I had perfect scores every time. I'm a real Annie Oakley, he said."

"Who was your husband?" Doyle asked.

"Max Wayne. He worked uptown."

Oscar's mouth dropped. "I heard of him, he was a real hero. Lots of busts and had a spotless record. You should be proud."

"Oh I am, it's so sad that he passed - cancer. It was hard, but he went quietly. Thank you for this opportunity to get back into life." She looked like she was going to tear up, so Doyle told her to go home and get ready for the morning.

She waved her hand and said she'd be in bright and early. Doyle said, "Leave the gun home, for now, just until we see how it goes."

She agreed and left.

"Wow, Max Wayne's wife. She must have some stories to tell. Well, should I tell anymore women coming in that we've filled the position?"

"Yep, I like her. I think we have our staff well picked." Doyle smiled. "Now we have to find Leo."

*

Chapter 11

"It would be a good idea to find him. Can't screw up our first case, it would look bad on our resume," Oscar said.

"Would be a bad omen, too. Let's see what we have on the man and start a plan," Doyle said.

"Would this be Plan B or Plan A?" Oscar mugged.

Doyle shook his head and mumbled, "Don't start with that now." He went to his desk and sat, pointing Oscar to the client chair. Oscar sat and leaned over to Doyle.

"He likes pool, we can show his picture around the pool halls," Doyle said.

"All of them?"

Doyle looked at his partner and said, "Yes, all of them, until we get a lead. Didn't you do any legwork as a police detective?"

"I tried to avoid it. But, since this is our business now, I'll do my best."

"Nice to hear. Then, he was a Mason, there's only one temple in the city. We can start there and hopefully they have him hidden away," Doyle said.

"I had an uncle who was a Mason, they're pretty secretive about their members. Too bad we can't get a warrant."

"We're not cops anymore, we don't need warrants now."

"And, I like that. We just bust heads now," Oscar said, too eagerly.

"There will be no head busting. We do it all legal-like. But, if it comes down to it, maybe one head." Doyle grinned at the thought. He had been written up in his past as a cop for busting heads, so it wouldn't bother him now that there was no one to write him up. "Shall we go to the temple first?"

They got up and went to the door. Doyle stopped and said, "We need Marge here to tell people we're out."

Oscar went to his desk and took a sheet of paper and wrote on it. He took some tape and brought the sign to the door, taping it to the back of the window. Doyle looked at it and smiled.

"*We are out detecting, be back later*," it said.

"That should work for now. Let's go," Doyle said and locked the door.

They got in Doyle's Charger and drove the short distance to Temple Street and Cass Avenue. Doyle drove around the back of the building and parked. They got out and stood by the car looking up at the tall structure.

"This is the largest Masonic Temple in the world, fourteen stories that house many chapters of Masonic-type organizations. They even house the Knights Templar." Doyle said.

"Wow, like in the *Indiana Jones* movie?" Oscar asked.

"Not quite the same, but of the same linage. I'm sure they don't hide the Ark of the Covenant or Christ's Holy Grail here. Then again, who knows?" Doyle smiled and walked to the entrance. Oscar followed, still mumbling about the Knights Templar.

They went in and up to a reception desk. Doyle smiled at the man seated at a desk. He got up and moved to them. "May I help you?"

"Yes, I'm Arthur Doyle and this is my associate, Oscar Drew. We're private investigators and we were hired by a young woman to find her missing father. He is a member of the Masons and I was wondering if there was someone we could talk to about him?"

"Well, we don't give out information about our members, but maybe our membership officer might have something for you." He wrote something on a piece of paper and said, "Go to this floor and room and ask for Jacob Holley. See if he can help you."

"Thank you, sir," Doyle said and looked around for the elevators. The man pointed down a hall and said to go that way.

They found the elevators and got on the first one that opened. There were fourteen floors to the building and the one they needed was on the twelfth. Doyle pushed the button and the car rose gently.

"Fancy place," Oscar said.

"This building has quite a history. I learned about it in school, in my history class about Detroit. There's so much mystery and theories about the Masons, even George Washington was a Mason, along with Ben Franklin."

"Did they plot world domination?" Oscar said with a smirk.

"Does it look like they took over the world?"

"Judging from the way our government works, I'd say they succeeded."

"I'll give you that," Doyle said as the car came to a stop and the doors opened. Doyle looked at the paper and noted the room number. They walked down the hallway in the direction the numbers were going and found the room.

"Do we have to know some secret knock to get in?" Oscar said. Doyle gave him a blank look, then opened the door.

There was a desk with a man seated behind it. "Are you the private eyes?" he asked. Doyle figured the reception desk man would call ahead.

"Yes, we are. I presume you are Jacob Holley. Did your cohort explain why we're here?"

Doyle's Law

"You're looking for a missing member. As you were told, we can't give out that sort of information.

"We were hired by his daughter, she's quite worried about him. We just need to know if he's been here in the last few days."

"This is a big building, sir. There are many amenities that a member could utilize. Swimming, tennis, any number of activities that I don't keep track of. Too many members, also."

"His name is Leo Kellogg, like the cereal. Does that ring a bell?" Doyle noticed the man's eyebrows flicker a little. He must have known the man or the name.

Holley turned to his computer and said, "If you can be discreet, I'll see what we have on Leo."

Doyle smiled and said, "We see nothing."

The man watched the screen and then said, "I'm sorry, but Leo hasn't checked in anytime in the last week. He was here back then to use the library."

Doyle wondered what Leo was after in the library. "Thank you for that much, it helps narrow down our investigation."

"Glad to help. I know Leo and he's a very nice man, other than his gambling problem. I hope you find him safe."

"We do, too," Doyle said and they thanked him and left the office.

They made it back to the car. Doyle stopped and leaned on the car top. "We need to split the pool halls to save time. Let's go back to the office and make a list of the halls around the city."

"What about the photo, we only have one," Oscar asked.

Doyle thought a moment and said, "Get in."

He drove out and went by a Walgreens he'd seen on the way to the temple. He parked and told Oscar to wait in the car. He went in and up to the photo center and asked the girl if she could make a couple copies of the Polaroid. She said she could and went to work on it. Ten minutes later, Doyle left with the copies. He handed one to Oscar and put the rest on the dashboard.

"Now we're all set," Doyle said and drove out.

They arrived back at the office and went in to get their phone book. They spent a short time writing down the names of all the pool halls in the city, dividing them between the east and west of the city.

"I live on the east side, so I'll take that area. You live on the west, that's your area," Doyle said. "We may as well spend the rest of the day searching. Go home after you've exhausted your search. We'll meet back here in the morning to get Marge set up."

"Works for me," Oscar said. He took his half of the list, said goodbye and went out the door.

Doyle watched his partner heading out, hoping he'd be alright. They still had permits to carry their weapons, so Oscar had protection. The pool halls on the west side weren't the best to go into, unless they knew you. Oscar made it this far as a cop, so he should be alright. Doyle liked Oscar, but never really knew much about the man until this last week as they worked to get the office set up.

Doyle's Law

Doyle was heading to the door when it opened and found a woman was standing there. "May I help you?" Doyle asked.

"Are you still hiring for the receptionist job?" she asked politely.

"Well, we have a woman who is going to do the job, but it's on a trial basis. Do you have a resume in case she doesn't work out?"

"I do," she said and opened her huge purse and took out a folder, giving it to Doyle.

"I'd talk to you right now, but I'm heading out to find a missing man. If she doesn't work out, I'll call you in for an interview."

"Thank you, I appreciate it." She turned and went out the still-opened door. Doyle watched her walk down the street and disappear. He went out the door and locked it.

He stood in front of the building, then walked towards Trumbull. He stopped on the corner looking across Trumbull at the large vacant lot that had a baseball diamond in the middle of it. Tiger Stadium once stood in the empty lot before they tore it down in favor of Comerica Park Stadium. Doyle's dad used to bring him there for the season openers. He would watch the Tigers win and lose games, never worrying about the standings. Doyle didn't care as long as he was with his father, it was special.

Now, the stadium was gone and so was his father. Memories were all he had now. He turned back to go to his car. He wanted to be sure Sara Kellogg had some time left with her father.

Chapter 12

There were two pool halls on Woodward and he decided to try both. They were fairly close to where Leo lived and he probably frequented them. The first was the *Fifth Avenue* in downtown Detroit. He got the directions from his GPS and drove there. It was a big building, nicely decorated. He parked and went in. The place was crowded for the time of day, which surprised him. He went to a table and sat watching the crowd. There seemed to be a tournament going on and the hustlers were falling fast according to the score board.

A waitress came to his table and he asked for a Miller in a bottle. She said they only serve beer in cans, saves on breakage. He agreed, she smiled and went off. He watched the men and some women shooting. It always amazed him at the precision of the shots, how they could bank the ball off the side to hit a ball across the table.

The waitress came back and Doyle paid her, then asked, "What's your name?"

She said "Val."

"Well, Val, I'm looking for a man."

She came back quickly, "This is the wrong bar, mister. The gay bars aren't in this neighborhood."

Doyle laughed and pulled his P.I. ID out and showed her. "I'm a private investigator and I'm looking for a missing man." He took the photo out and showed it to her. "Seen this man before?"

She looked closely and handed the photo back to Doyle. "Yeah, he's been in here, Leo is his name. Not lately though, maybe couple of weeks ago. He meets with his bookie when the creep is around."

"Why would a bookie meet with him here?"

"Hey, people take bets on everything, including pool. There's a lot of money under the table going on for this tourney. The bookies come around to collect or to pay out. Mostly collect."

"Are any bookies here right now? Especially one who dealt with Leo?"

"Sure, Louis is here. Leo used him a number of times." She pointed to man who was well dressed in a black sharkskin jacket and bolo tie around a pale blue shirt.

"Thanks, Val," Doyle said and tossed a ten on her tray. She smiled and said, "Anytime."

Doyle waited until the bookie, Louis, was alone. Doyle remembered the daughter saying she heard her father talking to a Louis on the phone about some money. Doyle downed the beer and went up behind Louis as the man stood watching the game on the main table.

Doyle leaned to the man and whispered in his ear. "I have a large Sig handgun aimed at your back. I just need to talk to you, so don't be a hero. I'm not afraid to shoot you in here. Shall we go out the back way?"

Louis whispered, "Okay, I'm no hero." Then he turned and headed for the back door. Doyle passed Val and gave her a wink. She smiled and said to come back any time. They went out the door to the back, which was deserted, other than trash dumpsters.

Doyle pushed Louis to the ground and pointed the Sig at him. "Hey man, I'll cooperate. As I said, I'm no hero."

"I hope you'll cooperate. I haven't beaten a man in over a month and I'm feeling the itch," Doyle growled.

"Hey, calm down, tiger. I'll do what you want."

Doyle moved closer and took out the photo and said, "You know this man, don't you?"

Louis looked at the photo and then said, "Sure, I know him, Leo Kellogg. He's into me for a tidy sum of money. He's a loser, man. I've been looking for him to pay up."

"Do you know where he is?"

"I said I was looking for him, I don't know where he is."

"Do you know any places he may be? Bars or other pool halls?"

"I've checked, and had my men looking for him, he's in the wind, as they say."

Suddenly, the back door flew open and out charged a large bruiser of a man, catching Doyle by surprise with his speed. Doyle turned just as the man brought his hand across Doyle's head, causing Doyle to spin to the ground. He still had the gun in his hand, but was at a bad angle to shoot. The man pounced on Doyle knocking the wind out of him. Doyle managed to bring his foot up to ward off another lunge by the brute. He kicked out and pushed the man back against the building, giving him time to stand and aim the gun at the man's leg and fired. The man screamed in pain and went down.

Doyle spun to see Louis standing now. "Going somewhere, Louie?" he said, aiming his gun at the bookie.

Louis looked to the behemoth on the ground in pain, holding his wound, Doyle moved around so he was facing the back door now.

"Louie, talk to me or you can join your gorilla on the ground." He aimed at Louis' leg and the man went pale.

"Okay, okay. I'll tell you what you want to know. I talked to Leo on the phone last week and he said he was getting some money to pay me off. He didn't say how, but said he would have it by yesterday. He never showed up."

"Anything else you remember?"

Louis was making a pained face, he was trying to think, Doyle presumed.

"Yeah, he said he had to go out of town, but would be back the next day. He said he had to go to Sterling Heights to meet a man. He said his luck was changing and would be able to pay me off."

"Did he say how his luck was changing?"

"No, that's all he said, I swear."

Doyle said, "You better take care of your buddy. I'll be back if I hear about you harassing Leo ever again. You'll be on the ground with a bullet in your gut. Understand?"

Louis nodded quickly and Doyle went by the man to the back door and in.

Val was standing by the bar and came over to Doyle as he made his way through the crowd. "Was that you making that loud noise out back?"

"I didn't frighten anyone, did I?" he replied.

"We're used to loud noises around here. What with the bookies scaring the losers, to the men pissed off at losing to a hustler. It gets noisy and the cops gave up coming around. You were a cop, right?"

"Does it show?"

"No, but I'm good at spotting them. I'm also good at being friendly to them."

Doyle caught her innuendo and grinned. "Well, Val, how friendly do you get?"

"Try me and see."

"Is this going to cost me?"

"Oh hell, no. I just like cops…and P.I.s like you. I'm no hooker."

Doyle took out a business card and wrote his apartment phone number on the back. "Look me up next time you are feeling friendly."

"I may call tonight," she said, looking at the card. "It's been a long while since there have been any good policemen in here."

"I'll be home." Doyle smiled and excused himself. "I have to go find Leo."

He walked away, still smelling her perfume. She was a looker, well built in a low cut tank top. Great ass, too. He hadn't had sex in over a month, since before Gwen left. Maybe his lonely streak was ending.

He got back in his car and pulled his cell phone to call Oscar. He waited for the phone to start ringing, then Oscar answered. "Any luck?" Doyle asked.

"Got a couple people who knew Leo, but no one knows where he's at. He's gone good according to these people. How about you?"

"I found the mysterious Louis from the phone call. Had a little run in with his goon, the goon will walk with a limp for a while, but Louis told me a few things about Leo. I'll explain tomorrow, I have a date tonight and I need to get ready for it."

"A date? Did you find some woman who is into self-abuse?"

"No, but one who has a thing for cops and P.I.s, and she's a looker."

"I guess going to the pool hall was good for you."

"Yep, and I didn't have to try hard."

"Well, be careful and don't forget to use a rubber. No telling what she has."

"You really know how to kill the mood, don't you?"

"I just don't want to hear you scream every time you take a pee," he said with a laugh. "I'm calling it a night and going home to self-abuse myself. See you in the morning." He hung up.

Doyle had a long day and wanted to go freshen up before Val showed. If she did. Some women are all talk. Either way, he wanted to be in bed early tonight, so he'd see if it was alone or with company.

Bob Moats

He drove down Woodward to the I-94 freeway ramp and then up to Moross where he cut over to Harper. He got to his apartment and went in to crash. He thought about cleaning his apartment, but decided the hell with it. He really didn't figure Val would want to get together with him, so he would kick off his shoes, grab a beer and watch some TV.

He was relaxing around seven when his phone rang. He answered and heard, "Is this the big strong P.I. that helps ladies in distress?"

"Depends on your distress."

"I got an itch that I can't reach. Can you scratch it for me?"

"Where are you?"

"In my apartment. I'll give you the address. Hurry, my itch is hurting."

She gave him the address and he said to give him twenty minutes. He hung up and thought, this is going to be a long night.

*

Chapter 13

The sun streamed in through the window onto Doyle's face. He twitched and turned his head to avoid the bright light. Then he opened his eyes and found he was in bed. He stretched and then looked around. It wasn't his bedroom. Then he remembered.

He sat up on the edge of the bed and saw his pants, underwear and socks on the floor. He dressed, but couldn't find his shirt. Doyle heard noise from another room and went to see what it was. He entered a hallway and then followed it to what was a living room. It looked well kept, nice furniture and decorations on the walls of various famous paintings. He was sure they were reproductions. Doyle heard the noise again and realized it was pots and pans. He looked around a corner into a kitchen and found a woman in his shirt. Then he remembered Val. How could he forget Val? She made him feel things he never felt before in bed with a woman. Doyle stood by the corner of the wall and coughed gently.

She turned her head to him and he saw she was strikingly beautiful, even in the early morning. Not that she wasn't beautiful last night, but he wasn't really concentrating on her face then.

"Good morning, tough guy. You slept well?"

"I did, thank you. Your bed is really comfortable."

"I hope I was comfortable, too." She went to him and put her arms around his body.

"Well, on a scale of one to ten, I'd say twelve. But, I could be coaxed into a few more numbers."

"Not this morning, hot one. I have to be into work early and so do you. You have a new receptionist to get set up."

That took Doyle by surprise. "Did I talk in my sleep?"

"No, but we had an interesting pillow talk. You told me a whole lot about your life and how you shot the mayor in the head. Nice move, smooth. I'd vote for you for mayor any day."

Doyle smiled and started to unbutton his shirt on her body. "I need this to go to work," he said as he pulled the shirt from her beautifully shaped naked body.

"Okay, maybe I can spare a little time to boost my numbers. Move it, stud." She turned him toward the bedroom and gave him a good push.

At seven-forty, Doyle arrived at the office and found Marge and Oscar waiting. "I'll get extra keys made for you, Oscar."

Oscar grinned and said, "Tough night, Art?"

"No, actually is was quite nice. I mean my night was very relaxing, I slept well," he said happily.

Doyle opened the door and stood back to let Oscar and Marge in. Marge smiled and said, "She did wonders for your mood."

Doyle's mouth dropped. He shut it up and followed them in and over to Oscar's desk. He said quietly, "Don't share my sex romps with Marge, okay?"

He smiled and said, "I said nothing. She just assumed it."

"Yeah, tell me another one." Doyle turned and went to Marge standing off to the side.

He looked around and realized she didn't have a desk. "Well, this is awkward." He looked to Oscar and said, "Another trip to the thrift shop."

He turned to Marge and said, "Use my desk until we get back. If anyone comes in, tell them to wait. We shouldn't be gone too long."

An hour later, they had a nice desk for Marge and a comfortable chair. She was happy and Doyle said they would gather the items she would need for the desk. They spent some time wiring a phone for her and she said that was good.

"Okay, you are set up to answer the phone, and if anyone comes in, find out if they need an investigator or if they are just slumming. Handle it however you feel."

"Don't worry, boss. I've been there before," she said and put her knitting bag on the desk. Doyle smiled and went back to his desk. Oscar was sitting in Doyle's client chair. Doyle stopped and looked around the room. "We need partition walls for privacy. I'll see what I can find." Doyle sat.

"Okay, enough office talk, tell me about the waitress," Oscar pushed.

"Nothing to tell, she was good...very good."

"Seeing her again?"

"I don't know. From the way she talked in the pool hall I figured she slept with a number of cops. But turns out she hasn't, or so she said. She was married to a cop, they had a not so nice marriage and a rough divorce and she said she didn't really like cops after that. But I intrigued her, so she played along. Amazing."

"Yep, she wants to make an honest man out of you and marry you," Oscar teased.

"Knock that off. I'm not ready for nor do I want to get married." Doyle looked over to Marge who was quietly knitting something. "Now, we need to find Leo."

"I got nothing but a few people who have seen him in the recent past. He did appear in the places I went to at least once since he was let out of prison. But, no one knows where he's at or what he was up to."

"Louis said he had come into some luck recently and had to visit someone in Sterling Heights. Do you know anyone in the Sterling PD that may have some info for us on criminal activities?"

"I know two men who are detectives. I'll call and see if they have anything on Leo, or a crime wave in the city."

"Good, if we can find a link, then maybe we'll find Leo," Doyle said.

"What's your girlfriend's name?" Oscar asked.

"Would you drop that," he said, then paused. "Val. If you must know."

"How was she? Come on, I don't have a life, talk to me," Oscar begged.

He looked over to be sure Marge was busy, she was into her knitting. He turned back to Oscar and said quietly, "She was fantastic. I've been with a small number of women, but never one like her. I could get used to her."

"Don't lose your edge now. Women can mess up your head," Oscar warned.

"I know, I've been going over my options all morning. I'll probably see her again if she wants. But no marriage, so don't bring it up again. Now, drop my sex life and get back to Leo."

"Let me call my friends in the Sterling Heights PD and see what they know."

"Good, we have work to do," Doyle said.

Oscar went to this desk to make the phone call while Doyle went to sit next to Marge. She put down her knitting. "If my knitting bothers you, I can stop."

"No, don't. This job will be boring at first, but I hope it will pick up as soon as we take on more clients and I do more advertising. Keep busy with your knitting, to give you something to do between clients. I have no problem with it."

"I hope I wasn't too forward with my comment about your private life. I just know when a man is happy from love."

"Well, there's no love yet. I don't even know where this will go, but I'm leaving my options open. If I ever seem crabby, let me know," he said with a smile. "How long were you married to Max?"

She sat back and smiled, probably thinking about her late husband. "We were married for almost fifty years. We were barely children when we fell in love.

I was seventeen and he was nineteen. Back then it wasn't so strange for teens to get married. They never expected people to live past thirty." She laughed. "Is she something special?"

"I have no idea, we just met."

"Ah, you need time to get used to each other," Marge said.

Doyle sat up and said, "Exactly, we hardly know each other." He went silent.

Marge waited then said, "She must be good in bed."

"Marge! That's personal," Doyle protested, shocked by the older woman's bluntness.

"I'm sorry, but you'll find I'm a very open and honest person. If you want a real opinion, I can be honest with you," Marge said, unabashedly.

Doyle laughed and said, "Okay, I'll accept that. You keep me in line." He stood and went back to his desk.

The front door opened and in walked Sara Kellogg. Marge asked if she could help her. Oscar came running over and said, "Marge, I got this, thanks."

He took Sara to his desk and had her sit. Doyle was watching the two of them. He knew that they needed walls.

"How are you doing, Sara?" Oscar asked.

"I'm holding up. Have you found anything about my father yet?"

"We've been doing our investigations. But nothing yet. We checked with the Masons, but he hadn't been there in a couple weeks. Do you know why he went to the Masonic library?"

She looked surprised. "No, I have no idea why he would go to a library, especially in the Masonic Temple."

"All right, we found Louis and he said your father had some good luck and had to go to Sterling Heights to see someone. Do you know who that might be?"

She looked more confused. "I don't know. He didn't tell me anything about getting lucky. I brought the phone bill to you," she said.

Oscar asked for it and she handed it to him. He looked at it and read the calls that were made recently. He had no idea who the numbers belonged to. He'd have to see if he could get someone in the phone company to give him the information.

"I hope this helps," she said.

"I'm sure it will. Thank you," Oscar replied.

*

Chapter 14

"How many of these numbers do you know? Let's eliminate them." He handed her a pencil and she looked at the bill.

She started from the top and scratched off any of the phone numbers she recognized. Oscar watched her until she got to the bottom. She handed the bill back to Oscar and he studied the twelve or so numbers left.

"Okay, six of these numbers are the same, I presume your father dialed them. The others are random numbers, could be anyone he called," he said, and put the bill down on his desk. "I'll check these numbers to see if they might help. Thank you for bringing this in, it will help I'm sure."

"My father still hasn't called. I hope he's all right."

"Maybe he's a little busy at the moment. I'm sure we'll find him, so go home and wait for our call."

"Thank you, Mr. Drew. I appreciate your help." She stood and Oscar took her to the front door and opened it for her. She thanked him again and left. Oscar went back to his desk as Doyle wandered over.

"You know, she's not too bad looking. Maybe you could ask her out for dinner. Looks like she could use a good meal," Doyle said.

"Okay, I'll stay out of your love life, you stay out of mine," Oscar said and picked up the phone bill. Doyle sat in Oscar's client chair and watched him. "These six numbers were all made early in the morning. Maybe he was going somewhere and was checking in. The calls were for less than two minutes, except this one, the last one made. It was over ten minutes."

He turned to his computer and brought up the website for the reverse phone number lookup. He entered the number in the box on the request form and hit enter.

"According to this, the phone number is in Sterling Heights," Oscar said.

"Does it show a name?"

"If I want the name, they charge me for that information. I hate these sites that lead you further into getting your info then want you to pay for it."

"Well, at least we know it's in Sterling Heights. Call your cop friends and maybe they can find out who owns the number."

Oscar pointed at Doyle and said, "Now that's something I hadn't thought of, thank you for that information," he said sarcastically.

Doyle grinned as Oscar pulled out his cell phone and looked up the number of the Sterling Heights Police. He found it and dialed the number from his desk phone. They had bought a couple business phones at the thrift shop that had speakers built in, so they could both listen to the conversation.

After a couple rings, a female voice came out from the phone, "Sterling Heights Police Department, how may I help you?"

"Well, the phone works," Oscar said quietly to Doyle. "Yes, I'd like to be connected to Detective Howard Jones. Tell him it's former Detective Oscar Drew."

The woman paused and said, "I'll connect you, hold one moment, please." She clicked off and they waited.

"Oscar, you old fart you. Are you retired now?" Jones said as he came on.

"Yep, got out while I was still alive. How's the suburbs treating you?"

"Fine, but your crime is spilling our way, stop it." He laughed. "What's up?"

"Well, I'm now a P.I. and working with former Detective Art Doyle. We have an office set up in the shadow of the old Tiger Stadium."

"Doyle? Isn't he the one who blasted the mayor, giving him a nice scar?"

"The very same," Doyle said. "I'm listening on the speaker."

"Hey Doyle, you couldn't have moved your sights an inch or two and took out the turkey with the perp?"

"Believe me, it's a shot I'll regret for a long time. I'm usually better than that."

Oscar said, "He's slipping, getting old. I need a favor Howie, can you look up a phone number for me?"

"Is it part of a crime investigation? They're getting strict around here about using the system for personal needs. Too many cops looking up girlfriends," he said with a laugh.

"We have an ex-con who went missing three days ago. His daughter hired us to find him. We have a phone number that he called a number of times before he disappeared."

"Okay, that sounds official. What's the number?"

Oscar told him and Howard said to wait. He came back and said, "Give me your number, our computer guy is out and I don't want to play with the phone program. He's touchy about it."

"Sure, I can do that," he replied and gave him the office number and his cell phone number.

"Great, I'll call when I have something. Talk later." He hung up.

"Don't they trust the detectives to look up numbers?" Doyle asked.

"They have a different hierarchy out in the suburbs. Everything has to be by the book. Not like Detroit, where it was haphazard. Hold on." Oscar went to his laptop and punched a few keys then smiled. "I'm in."

"In what?" Doyle asked.

"The DPD database. A year ago, I had our computer IT guy fix my laptop so I could get into the database. I still have my password and apparently they didn't lock me out when I left. This is great, we can look up perps now."

"Let me try that, to see if I can still get in."

Oscar logged out and turned the laptop towards Doyle. He entered his password into the form and a big box popped up with big red letters saying "ACCESS DENIED" and the letters were flashing.

Oscar laughed and said, "Cadeem must have wiped you out completely. You are no longer welcome."

"Fat-assed jerk," Doyle said. "Well, at least you can still get in. Just use it sparingly, so they don't notice."

"Will do. Now, we wait for Howie to call with a name. I'll call the other single numbers to see who they are," Oscar said.

"Use the caller ID block feature so they don't get our number. I'll go get some office supplies for Marge, and I need to pick up some things, also." Doyle stood.

"Don't forget to buy a big box of condoms," Oscar said quietly.

Doyle ignored him and went to Marge. "Feel like coming along to get you some supplies?"

She put her knitting down and grabbed her purse. "Love to." She stood as Doyle told Oscar he was taking Marge. Oscar waved as he was dialing numbers.

Doyle took Marge to his car. "Oh, a nice Dodge Charger, what year?"

"2010, the police interceptor model. I keep it in good shape." They got in and Doyle started it.

Marge noticed switches on the dash with the words, "Flashers" and "Siren" and she asked, "Do those work?"

Doyle grinned and flipped the siren switch. The thing blared out loudly, causing people nearby to jump.

"I love it. Max never took me in his patrol car. I missed out on the fun. You can't use these legally, can you?"

"No, I'm not a cop anymore so they are there for fun. Maybe to pull over a perp one day." He drove out and went up Trumbull over the Fisher Freeway and across to Temple Street. He pulled into B&C Supply that had everything they would need. Doyle and Marge went in and he told her to grab whatever she felt she would need to do her job. She scampered off while Doyle wandered around looking at the aisles of office stuff.

He was in an aisle that had a small opening towards the front of the store. He saw a younger man behind the counter looking frightened and noticed another man was pointing a gun at him. Doyle moved quietly around the aisle and drew his Sig. He snuck up quietly behind the armed man and brought his gun to the man's neck.

"I would suggest you freeze and put your gun down on the counter. My trigger finger is really itching to fire this gun."

The robber stiffened and looked in the mirror behind the counter and saw Doyle. He took on a look of terror and slowly lowered the gun to the counter. Doyle brought his gun back and cracked it across the robber's head. The man dropped down to the floor.

Marge was coming around with her arms filled with supplies. She saw the man on the floor and the gun on the counter. "Damn, did I miss something?"

"Have the nice man ring us up before he calls the police," Doyle told Marge. She put the stuff on the counter and the man bagged everything and handed the bag to Doyle saying, "It's on the house. Thank you so much."

"Keep the gun handy in case he wakes before the police get here." They left the store.

"Aren't you going to stay around to explain to the police what happened?" Marge asked outside the building.

"Nope, too much paperwork will need to be filed, then they'll want to check my gun permit and I don't want to deal with police right now. I'll be the Lone Ranger and ride off into the sunset after saving the town from the Cavendish gang."

"I see you are a fan of the Lone Ranger. I used to listen to the show on the radio, then I watched it on TV. The original Lone Ranger, Clayton Moore."

Doyle could hear a police siren and said, "Get in, we need to make our escape."

Marge smiled and said, "You got it Kemo Sabe."

Doyle laughed and started the car.

*

Chapter 15

On the way back to the office, Marge spoke, "I remember when most of these streets were safe. When I was a young girl and could walk around without fear of being harmed. Now the city is getting worse. At least away from the city center, where they take care of their city jewels and the casinos. I was always in fear for Max every time he went out the door in the morning. Would he get shot in a bust gone bad? The city can eat you up. All the drug users and those who rob for a fix. That incident back there is how easy it is to be involved in a robbery."

"There's still some good to the city. I saw it when I was a cop. The bad stuff gets more notice. What happened back there was just one out of a thousand times you could go in that store without seeing a robbery. We were in the right place at the wrong time."

"So was the robber," Marge said, smiling.

They arrived back at the office and went in. Marge went to work getting her desk set up. Doyle went to Oscar's desk and sat in the client chair. "So, how did your calls go?"

"Very interesting and I may have an answer as to what Leo was up to. Why his luck was turning."

"Okay, talk to me."

"Two of the phone calls were made to party stores. Not strange, but as I was talking to the cashier, or whoever it was at the first store, I found that most people who call the store just want to get the lottery numbers. Leo called two different stores. You think maybe he was getting a second opinion as to the numbers?" Oscar paused for effect. "The last phone number I called was to the lottery commission office in Detroit. Now I have a feeling that Oscar had a lucky ticket."

"That would be a lucky break for him. And a reason to disappear with his winnings," Doyle said.

"Or, someone made him disappear to take his ticket," Oscar added. "Being murdered is the only way I would give up my winnings."

"I hope for Sara's sake that didn't happen."

"We need to find out who recently won big in the lottery," Oscar said.

"Which one? Hell, there's a dozen types of lotteries in Michigan. The state wants every dime they can get," Doyle said.

"If someone did do in Leo for his winnings, it would have to be a lot of money. Last week, the Mega Millions lottery came in at fifteen million. The Powerball was over one-hundred million. That's a good motive to murder. Even if he had one of the lower prize tickets, he still would have a cool million."

Doyle smiled. "And you know all these figures, how?"

"Hey, I get tickets every week. When I hit big I'm taking you out for dinner," Oscar said with a grin.

"Big spender, thanks," Doyle mugged. "The lottery winners are public info, so we shouldn't have much trouble finding out who won recently. When do you think he had the winning ticket?" Doyle asked.

"Well, the first call to a party store was last Saturday, the day after the Mega Millions. The Powerball was Wednesday and he would have called Thursday."

"Unless he didn't realize he had the winning ticket."

"True, but if he's like me, I'm checking right after the day they draw the numbers, so I think he had a Mega Million ticket."

"Well then, we need to find out who brought in the winning ticket that day," Doyle said, "Then maybe we'll have a suspect."

"I'll get the address and we can go." Oscar pulled the phone book and looked. "It's not far."

"Great, shall we go and find out?" Doyle stood and went to Marge. "We're going out, if anyone is looking for help, ask them to either wait or leave a number. We may be gone a while." She nodded her understanding and Doyle went out followed by Oscar.

They drove over to the lottery office and went in. The woman at the counter behind the plate glass asked what they needed. She was a huge, round-faced black woman in her forties. She didn't look happy. Doyle held up his ID and said, "We need to know who the winners were last week for the Mega Millions. We're tracking the possible theft of the winning ticket."

The woman stared and then said, "Which one? There were five winners in the draw. They all had winning tickets and share in the win."

Doyle looked at Oscar. "This is going to be complicated." He turned back to the woman and asked. "Can we get the list of winners?"

"You'll have to see the director to get those. I don't have them," she replied.

"Okay, where do we find him?"

"Her. I know it might be odd to you, but women can actually hold prominent positions these days. Oh, and in case you didn't know, we can actually vote now, too," she said sarcastically.

"Voting, huh? You don't say. Well, I'll be damned," Doyle exchanged the sarcasm lightheartedly. So, where can we find her?" Doyle asked, grinning.

The woman rolled her eyes, pointing to a door on the right and said, "Go through there and ask for Melody Connelly."

"Thank you," Doyle said and the men went to the door. It was locked. He looked back to the woman, she smiled, pressing a button. The door buzzed and Doyle opened it.

"I think she likes you," Oscar said.

"Shut up," Doyle said back.

Doyle's Law

They went to a woman at a desk in the lobby. "We'd like to see Melody Connelly," Doyle stated politely.

"Do you have an appointment?" she asked.

"No, we just have a couple questions to ask." Doyle showed his ID and then said, "We need some info on a recent winner."

"Hold on, I'll see if she's available." She picked up a phone and made a call. She talked and listened, then hung up. "She'll be with you shortly."

"Thank you," Doyle said.

Doyle walked around the lobby checking out the photos of past winners on the walls. There were hundreds of them, covering three walls. Oscar was chatting up the receptionist as her phone rang. She answered and said, "You can go in now."

They thanked her and entered the door she pointed to. They entered a large office, well decorated and plush furniture. Lottery money at work, Doyle thought.

The woman behind the desk stood and said, "I'm Miss Connelly, how may I help you?"

Doyle took her extended hand and said, "I'm Arthur Doyle, and this is my associate, Oscar Drew. We're private investigators looking for a missing man. His daughter hired us to find him, and in our investigating we deduced that he may have had a winning ticket for last Friday's Mega Million. Unfortunately, the man has vanished and his daughter is worried."

"I can tell you if he turned in the ticket, although they haven't awarded the money yet," she said, motioning to the chairs in front of her desk. They sat.

"We're hoping he did, but there are circumstances that lead us to believe he may have been harmed for the ticket. The man's name was Leo, or Leonard, Kellogg, like the cereal."

"Interesting name and one I don't remember having turned in a ticket."

"I was wondering if we could get a list of the winners to narrow down one person who may be our suspect."

"Names of winners are public, so I can give you that, but nothing else."

"Could you see your way to give us the cities they live in?" Doyle asked. "Just to narrow down the search."

She sat thinking. "I could do that." She turned to her computer and punched the keys. She stared at the screen on her monitor and said, "There is one winner from Traverse City and one from Grand Rapids. The rest are from the Detroit area. I can print out these names with cities for you. Would that help?"

"Yes, we would appreciate it," Doyle answered.

She hit a couple keys and the printer on a cabinet behind her started up, clattering as it pulled the paper from the tray. The thing spit out the sheet as the woman turned to retrieve it. She glanced at it to make sure it was complete. She turned back and reached out to Doyle with the sheet. He stood and took it.

"I hope that helps find your man. I've had other investigators, both private and police in here looking for winners who may have not been the original owners of the tickets. So this is nothing new. Good luck with your search."

Oscar stood next to Doyle as Doyle thanked her and they turned to go out. They went through the lobby and out to the front where Oscar waved to the woman behind the glass. She rolled her eyes again.

"Now there's a woman who needs a man," Oscar said with a grin out on the sidewalk in front of the building.

"She'd probably crush him," Doyle said as he looked at the printout. "As she said, there are two from outstate, they wouldn't be of use. The other three are from Mt. Clemens, Warren and Detroit. None from Sterling Heights. Did you ever hear back from your buddy about the phone number?"

"Oh, yeah, sorry I forgot. He said it had to be a burn phone, it's wasn't listed in the phone company register."

"Figures, damn cheap cell phones. The closest winner to Sterling Heights is in Warren. Shall we go there first?"

They got back to the car, drove out and back to the office to see if they could get an address for the winner. Marge was busily knitting and said they had no visitors.

They went to the phone book and looked up the name, Daniel Foster. Doyle found one listed in Warren and wrote down the address and phone number. He picked up the desk phone and dialed the number after blocking the caller ID. A male voice answered and Doyle said, "Mr. Foster, I'm Bill Russo from the Detroit News and I'd like to interview you about your win in the Mega Millions."

Doyle waited and the man finally said, "I guess that would be all right, sure."

*

Chapter 16

Doyle wrote down the address and directions to Foster's house. He hung up and said, "Shall we go play reporters?"

"Hold on," Oscar said and took a nice Nikon camera out of his desk. "Now I look like your photographer."

"Good idea, we get a photo of him that way. Let's go." Again, Doyle told Marge they were going out. The drive up to Warren took about a half hour in the traffic, and another ten minutes driving around to find the house in the subdivision. They parked out front and went to the house.

"We're right on the border of Warren and Sterling Heights. Maybe Leo was confused about the city," Oscar said.

"Could be, we'll find out soon enough," Doyle said as he knocked on the door to the house.

Doyle's Law

After a few moments the door opened and a rather small man stood there.

"Mr. Foster? I talked to you on the phone about the Mega Millions," Doyle said.

The man opened the door and invited them in. He went into another room that could have been a family room. He asked them to sit.

"Thank you, Mr. Foster," Doyle said as he introduced themselves to the man as Bill Russo and Dale King. "I'm sure you're delighted to have won in the lottery, even if you have to share with four others."

"Any amount of money is welcome. I would have liked to have taken all of it, but I'm not greedy. You said you're from the Detroit News?"

"Actually, we're freelancers. We write Op-Ed pieces and special interest articles for both the Free Press and the News. We came across your win through a friend. Leo Kellogg?"

Doyle watched his face and he made no flicker of recognition. His face remained unchanged.

"I don't know the man. Does he know me?"

"He's one of our contacts who finds interesting pieces to write about. Where he gets his info is not known to us."

"You don't check his sources?"

"That's why we called you on the phone to verify you had won in the lottery. Now, just where did you buy your ticket?" Doyle took out his notepad and pen to look official.

Foster smiled and said, "From the party store on the corner across Fourteen Mile Road. Luigi's, they

106

make great pizza and subs also. I go there a lot. Luigi was delighted when I told him I had won. You know he gets a percentage of the prize also."

"Well, I would say that would make him happy." Doyle was feeling pretty sure this man wasn't a suspect.

Foster stood, went to a desk, picked up a photo and gave it to Doyle. "Here's a photo that was taken at Luigi's when I told them about the winning ticket."

Doyle studied the photo. It showed two men standing in front of a deli counter, holding a piece of paper. There was a daily tear-off calendar on the wall. It was showing as last Saturday. Leo disappeared on Monday, so Foster had the ticket before Leo called the Lottery people.

"We're holding a photocopy of the ticket. I had it locked away safely, never can be too sure of people."

"Really, do you still have the photocopy?"

Foster went and got the paper and brought it to Doyle. "Why don't you hold this in front of you while my partner gets a shot with his camera?"

"Of course, where shall I pose?"

"On the couch will be good," Oscar said and brought the Nikon up and aimed it at Foster. The man smiled as Oscar snapped a couple pictures of him holding the photocopy.

"What do you plan to do with the winnings?" Doyle asked.

"I'm putting most of it in the bank and then taking a world tour. I've already talked to a travel agent. Ten countries in thirty days. I'm excited."

Doyle's Law

Doyle was doodling on the note pad to look like he was taking notes. He was actually writing Val over and over. He looked up to see Oscar finished taking a number of shots.

"I think we've taken up enough of Mr. Foster's time, Dale. Shall we go?"

"I've got a couple good shots, I'm good to go," Oscar said, looking at the small preview screen of the camera.

Doyle stood and said, "I'm not sure if or when this will be put in the paper, it's up to the editors, but thank you for cooperating." Foster walked them to the door, thanking them as they left.

On the sidewalk walking to the car, Doyle said, "Not him. Damn."

They sat in the car, organizing their thoughts. "We have two other local names to check. Since we're up this way, we can go to Mt. Clemens for the second winner." Doyle took out the paper that the lottery woman gave him and looked it over. Then he said, "Here's something interesting. On the bottom of the list in small print, there's a disclaimer from the lottery bureau. It says '*These winners are 5 of 6 appearing in the search of same ticket numbers issued as the winning number. It is the responsibility of the ticket holders to report their tickets to the commission to claim their winnings.*' So we don't have the complete list. There's one more out there. Crap."

"Would have been nice of the lottery woman to have told us," Oscar said. "Still want to go to Mt. Clemens?"

"I don't think so. We can call these people and get as much info from them. Let's go back to the office, after I make one stop."

Doyle drove out of the subdivision and found a small hardware store. He pulled in and told Oscar that he'd be right back. About ten minutes later, he came back and opened a small bag, pulling out a key. He handed it to Oscar. "Now you can let yourself in the office in the morning." He handed the bag to Oscar and said, "There's an extra one for Marge, give it to her."

Doyle drove back to the office and they found Marge still knitting. "I hope you don't get too bored here, Marge," Doyle told her.

"No, but a radio would be nice to have," she said. "Just for background music."

"I'll bring one in tomorrow," Doyle said and went to his desk. He thought about calling Val to see what she was up to. Maybe they could get together tonight to relive last night and this morning. Doyle wasn't going to get greedy, but she was really good for his libido. He dialed her number and it rang for a long time. He was starting to think she might be at work when the phone was lifted. He heard something in the background, a man yelling, "Don't answer that, you bitch, put the phone down." He heard a quiet voice, Val's saying, "Help me." Then the phone went dead.

Doyle jumped up yelling to Oscar, "I'll be back, something has come up." He was out the door before Oscar could respond, and in his car heading out. The apartment building wasn't too far, but he was rushing. He thought about using the flashers and siren, but he didn't need to get stopped by a real cop right now.

He drove into the parking lot and came to a quick stop. He jumped out and ran into the building, up to her apartment. He could hear a man yelling and calling names. He pounded on the door until it opened. Val was standing there. She had a bruise on her cheek and a cut lip.

"What the hell," Doyle said just as the door was pulled open wider. There stood a man about an inch taller than Doyle and almost as muscular.

"Who the hell are you?" the man barked. Then he grabbed Val's hair and pulled her away from the door. She screamed as Doyle sprang at the man with the flat fist of his right hand, driving it into the man's throat. The brute staggered back and then recovered as Doyle stood just inside the doorway. The crazed man charged Doyle, he sidestepped, tripped him and the jerk crashed to the floor. He fell out into the hallway as Doyle turned towards him. He jumped up and Doyle charged him, bringing his arm and elbow into the man's neck, pinning him to the wall. The man gave Doyle a punch to the ribs causing Doyle to fall back. He took another a swing at Doyle and caught the side of Doyle's head, spinning him around and back into the apartment.

Doyle was on the floor and being kicked by the brute. Doyle was trying to protect his head and private areas. The man was walking around Doyle, still kicking, when Doyle heard a clang and a crack.

He looked up to see Val with a cast iron skillet in her hands and the man dropping to the ground.

"Son-of-a-bitch!" she yelled. Then she started pummeling him with the skillet. Doyle jumped to his feet and took the skillet away as she fell into his arms and cried profusely.

Doyle looked at the man unconscious on the floor and said, "Your ex, I presume?"

She nodded her head then pulled back. "He had a restraining order to stay away, a lot good that did."

Doyle took her to the couch and sat her down. He pulled two plastic zip-cuffs from his jacket pocket and secured the man's hands and feet. He asked Val if she had the restraining order handy. She said she did. He pulled his cell phone and made a call.

"Marco, Art Doyle here. I have a small problem. Maybe you can help."

*

Chapter 17

Forty minutes later, there were two uniformed officers and a detective at the apartment. The detective was Marco Lupis, a friend of Doyle's from another precinct.

"Do you have it?" Doyle asked in the hallway.

"Yep. I'll plant it before they frisk him. He'll regret messing with us. He's a former cop, you know."

"Yeah, I've heard all about him. Kicked from the force for being an asshole and fighting with other cops. I don't know what Val saw in him."

"He's big and strong. You didn't take him down, your lady friend did," Marco said with a grin. "You were cringing on the floor."

"Keep that to yourself, please. I won't tell that you're planting drugs on him."

"Deal, now let's go take care of our perp." Marco went in ahead of Doyle and told the officers to stand him up. As they were lifting him from the front, Marco stuffed a bag of coke in his back pocket. They held him up as he was coming around. Marco told the officers to search him.

"What the hell?" he said as he gathered his wits. Marco came around front and said, "You're under arrest for domestic assault, violating a restraining order and attacking this man. He's pressing charges."

One cop came around and said, "Lieutenant, look at this." He held out the bag of coke.

"Well, I have to figure that we have you for possession, too. I'd say that's a good eight ounces of coke. That will set you up in a nice cell for a long while."

"What the…that's not mine. I don't know where that came from. I'm being railroaded!" he protested.

"Tell it to the judge. Cut his feet loose and take him to the car. Be careful, he's dangerous. If he resists arrest, add that to his charges after you beat him senseless."

The uniforms both smiled and led him out. He was still yelling about being set up. Marco went to Val and said, "You'll have to file charges. Art told me he used your camera to take photos of your face. It should help put him away on the abuse." He looked to Doyle and said, "I'm sure you have the situation in hand now. Can I leave you here without her hitting you with the skillet?"

Val and Doyle both laughed and said they'd be fine. Marco said, "You owe me one, Doyle." Then he left.

"Drugs? Ken never used drugs. So where would he get them?" she asked.

"Haven't the foggiest idea. Maybe after he left you he was so despondent that he got into drugs," Doyle said coyly.

"Whatever, as long as it puts him away for a long time. Away from me." She put her arms around Doyle and kissed him, then she jumped. "Ow, my cut hurts."

"Let's get you fixed up so you can relax." He led her to the bathroom where he proceeded to put astringent on her cut and a cold water rag on her bruise. She sat on the closed toilet.

"I heard a knocking and thought it might be you. I shouldn't have opened the door before I looked out the peephole. He barged in and started with his crap about whether I was seeing other men. I warned him about the restraining order then he started hitting me.

She lifted her blouse and Doyle could see more bruises around her ribs.

"Hold on. I'll get the camera and record those." He went to get the camera and came back. He finished taking the pictures. "I think you need to get naked so I can record every possible bruise."

"You mean besides the ones you gave me. I bruise easily."

"I'll remember that. I can be rough without leaving bruises."

They went to the living room and sat on the couch getting a second wind. Val rested her head on his chest and thanked him. "Are you always going to be around to protect me?"

"No, but I'll see you have a gun for the next time," he said.

"I hope there won't be a next time."

Doyle's cell phone rang and he looked at the caller ID, it was Marco. "What's up?" He listened for a moment then said, "Well, that settles that, thanks for the heads up." He hung up.

"What?" Val asked.

"Seems that when they got to the precinct, Ken had managed to break the zip-cuff and grabbed a uniform, pulling his gun. He wasn't being very bright with a dozen cops around him. He held them off and then he shot at another cop who got too close, just winged him, but Ken was shot by another cop." Doyle paused. "He's dead."

"I guess I won't have to worry about him now," she said quietly.

Doyle thought, justice is met.

Bob Moats

Doyle stayed the night to be sure Val was all right. He got up extra early to go to his apartment to change clothing. Not good to go into work wearing the same clothing as the day before. He had to remember to get a radio for Marge. Val was sleeping soundly as he dressed, then he left her a note. He slipped out the door being sure it was locked and went to his car.

At seven-forty, Doyle arrived at the office and found Oscar and Marge at their desks. "You know you don't have to be in here until eight," he said going to his desk, placing the boom box down. He removed his jacket and took the boom box to a ledge next to Marge's desk and plugged it in. "You can select whatever music you want as long as it's not rap."

Marge thanked him and he went to Oscar's desk. "Tough night? What happened? You ran out of here and I had no idea what was going on," Oscar inquired.

Doyle sat and relived the story of his adventure in Val's apartment. He finished and Oscar said, "You live this life that others only dream of. Taking down a robber and then an abusive ex-husband. Well, he's dead, so your field is wide open."

"Not the way I wanted to start a relationship with a woman. With a dead ex."

"Relationship? You decided this is going to be a relationship?"

"I like her, and she has some great attributes. I could get used to her."

"Don't forget the rubbers," Oscar laughed.

Doyle's Law

Doyle made a noise with his tongue and stood. "I can't win around you." He went to his desk.

Doyle was enjoying the music Marge had selected, classic rock, and was going over his paperwork for expenses of the last couple days. Everything would be needed for tax time.

The front door opened and in came Sara Kellogg. Doyle stood and went to her. "Sara, is there something you need?"

"I need to talk to the both of you," she said quietly. He led her back to Oscar's desk and had her sit. He pulled over another chair and sat in front of her.

"Okay, what is it you need to tell us?" Oscar asked.

She opened her purse and took out an envelope. She opened it and took out a piece of paper that looked like a check or money order. "I went shopping last night for food, when I got back I found this was on the floor just inside my door." She handed it to Doyle and he looked at it. He handed it to Oscar and he whistled.

"One-hundred-thousand dollars, made out to you. It's a bank check, so there's no signature."

"Nothing else, no note explaining who left this?" Doyle asked.

"I have no idea who left it or where it came from," she replied.

Doyle looked at Oscar, "Gift from her father?"

"Or guilt money from someone else."

"I'm sure you want to cash this, but may I keep the envelope?" Doyle asked.

"You can have it. I'm afraid to go cash it. What if I get robbed?"

"Where do you bank?" Oscar asked.

"I have a credit union that I bank with."

Oscar looked and saw where the check was issued and said. "I'll take you to get it cashed and we can go put it in your bank."

"That would be so nice of you to do that. With this money I can pay you for your services now."

Doyle smiled and said, "We can discuss that later, we need to solve this first, then we can settle up." He turned to Oscar and said, "Go ahead and take her out. I'm hanging around today."

Oscar stood and took Sara to his car and drove out.

Doyle held the envelope carefully, hoping there may be fingerprints on it. But, who would he call to have it examined? The forensic people were in the same building as Cadeem and he didn't want to run into him. Maybe when Oscar got back, he could take it in. That would work. He put the envelope into a bigger one and put it on Oscar's desk.

He sat at his desk wondering who would send Sara that much money. The missing sixth person with the winning ticket hadn't turned it in yet, so where would they get the money from? Leo said he had to go see a man in Sterling Heights. Maybe this man was a benefactor who gave Leo money for the ticket and Leo sent the money to his daughter for all the pain he caused her over the years. Too many angles to think of. He needed to find the Sterling Heights man and find out the connection.

His head was hurting a little from the whack Ken gave him. He popped a couple aspirin from his desk, then sat back and relaxed.

*

Chapter 18

Doyle was at his desk when Oscar came back in. Doyle looked up at his partner and asked, "You look serious, did everything go well at the banks? Did you get her settled in?"

"Sure, everything went really smooth." Oscar paused then went to the chair next to Doyle. "I dropped off Sara at her car out back, and I had the radio on. The news came on and I heard a report about a big house fire in Warren, total loss. They said the name of the owner. It was Foster's house, and they said he was in it."

Doyle felt a chill and sat back in his chair. "When did this happen?"

"The news said it happened about two hours ago. They're sifting through the rubble to find a cause for the fire. I called a friend of mine in the Warren FD and he said they think it was deliberately set. The fire inspector hasn't concluded his findings yet, but my friend said it was a good bet that someone torched the place."

"Well, that's one winner down. Maybe we need to talk to the others," Doyle said.

"Foster seemed like a nice man, this is so wrong." Oscar stood up next to Doyle and waited.

Doyle took the list from his pocket and studied it. "We need to find these people. This one in Detroit, can you look in the book and see if she's listed?"

"She?"

"The name is Brandy, I'd say it's a woman. Take a look and see if you can find her. If not, call any more of the many friends you have that may help. I don't want to see another murder."

Oscar took a look at the list, noted the name and went to his desk. He opened the phone directory and went through it. "I found a Brandy Williams who lives on Beaubien, near Mack Avenue. I've got the address."

"Shall we go?" Doyle said, standing. "Oh, and take that brown envelope on your desk. I need you to go to forensics and see if they can get any prints off the envelope that Sara got the check in."

"Worried about Cadeem finding you if you go into forensics?"

"Something like that," Doyle smiled. "Marge, we're off again."

She waved from her knitting and Doyle led Oscar out. They drove over and found an apartment building. Oscar said, "The address didn't include an apartment number."

Doyle's Law

"We'll find the building Super and see what he says." They parked near a sign that designated where the office was and went to the front door. They went in and found two desks, one with a man, the other with a woman, seated.

The woman stood and went to them. "May I help you?"

"I'm Art Doyle and this is Oscar Drew. We're private investigators and we're looking for Brandy Williams. Could you direct us to her apartment?"

The woman looked upset and said, "I'm sorry, but Brandy was found dead yesterday in her apartment. A friend found her. The police investigated and sealed up the apartment. That's all I can tell you."

Doyle was feeling lost now. Two dead lottery winners. He looked to Oscar and said, "We need to talk to the police, now."

Oscar agreed and they thanked the woman. Back out at the car they stood. "Who should we talk to?" Oscar asked.

"Other than Cadeem, we still have friends on the force. Let's find out who has this jurisdiction and talk to them. Maybe he gave his card to the manager woman. Run back in and see."

Oscar went off as Doyle stood waiting. He was feeling at a loss and didn't like it. Sometimes having a case that solves itself was good. He was concerned for the other ticket holders. Even the ones in Traverse City and Grand Rapids. When he was a cop, something like this would be easy to work out. He had the whole police department to help. From forensics to the computer people who could find things fast. Now as a private investigator he had to think for himself and work it out without the extra help.

He was watching the office and saw Oscar coming back. Oscar came up and showed Doyle the business card the detective gave the manager. Doyle read the name and smiled. "Good, I know this detective, he's decent. If we share our info with him he should be able to get something moving. Let's go to his precinct and have a talk."

They got into the car and drove out. Fifteen minutes later, they arrived at the east side precinct and went in.

The desk officer saw them and smiled at the men. "Well, the two bad boys of the 4-6, shoot any new public officials? Does Cadeem know you're slumming?"

"You evidently haven't heard that we quit the force. We're private now," Oscar said.

"And Cadeem is the least of our worries," Doyle added.

"Well, that's great. Who you looking for here?"

"Harry Lowe. Is he in?" Doyle asked.

"I'll check, hold on," he said and made a call. He finished the call and said, "He's in back. We have the same floor plan as the 4-6. So look for homicide."

"Thanks," Doyle said and they went through a door into the building.

Other than the people, it was just like their old precinct. They wandered through the hallways and found the Homicide squad room. Doyle asked an officer where Lowe was.

He pointed to a cubicle and they thanked him. Doyle admired the cubicle walls and still thought about getting them for the office.

Doyle looked over the wall of the cubicle and saw Lowe at his desk. "Are there any good detectives around here?" he said.

Lowe jumped, then looked up. "Damn you, Doyle. I was deep in thoughts about a gruesome murder and you scared the crap out of me."

Doyle came around the partition to the opening. "These are nice walls. Where'd you get them?"

"They came with the job. Do you want yours back?"

"Hell, no. I'm fine on my own, now. I've gone private and I'm working my first case, a missing man. His disappearance may have something to do with your case on Brandy Williams."

"How'd you know about that?" Lowe asked.

Doyle reached over and grabbed Oscar by the arm and pulled him over. "This is my partner, Oscar Drew. We went to the apartment building where the late Brandy Williams lived to talk to her and found out through the manager that she was dead. We got your name from them."

"Sorry that you're saddled with this lug, Oscar. What's Brandy have to do with your case?"

"Aren't you going to ask us to come in and sit?" Doyle said.

Lowe pointed to his chairs and the men went in the cubicle and sat.

"Our missing man may have had a winning ticket in last Friday's Mega Millions. We got a list from the Lottery people and Brandy was on it. We didn't go visit her yet, we went to another winner in Warren. Daniel Foster. He was burned to death in a house fire today. Now, we find that the second name on the list, your Brandy, is also dead. I don't like coincidences, but this sounds like one to me."

"How many winners are on the list?" Lowe asked.

"There were five, three in this area and two outstate, Traverse City and Grand Rapids. There's one left in Mt. Clemens, but we don't know where he lives. Thought you might like to tie up the coincidence."

"Give me the name and I'll call the Sheriff's office up there. Mt. Clemens doesn't have a police force anymore, couldn't afford them. So, the Sheriff's took over. You think someone is murdering the winners to take the whole pot?"

"Well, as it turns out, there was a sixth winning ticket bought. According to their computers. But the winner hasn't turned in the ticket yet. We think it may have something to do with our missing man." Doyle handed Lowe the list. "Copy off the remaining names, you can get some action on this better than we can."

"The joys of being a cop. But, you don't have to worry about that now," Lowe said. "How's business?"

"We just started, so only one woman looking for her missing father. Can you let us know what you find out?" He handed Lowe his business card.

"I'll call as soon as I have some word. Good to see you again, and to meet you, Oscar."

Doyle and Oscar stood and thanked him again. They went back out to the car and Doyle drove out.

"Now what?" Oscar asked.

"We wait. Not much more we can do without the name of the missing winner. I'm thinking it has something to do with Leo. I also think that the winner won't come forward until the others are all dead and he or she will wait until the heat dies down. These ticket holders have so many days before they have to turn in their tickets."

They drove back to the office and went in. Marge was on the phone, saw them and finished up. "That was someone from the lottery office, they had another winner turn up. You left your card and the woman I talked to said she thought it may help."

Doyle looked at Oscar, "The suspense is building." He looked back to Marge and asked, "Did she give a name?"

Marge picked up a piece of paper and handed it to Doyle. He looked at it and sighed.

Oscar asked, "Well, what does it say?"

"Sara Kellogg."

*

Chapter 19

"What?" Oscar exclaimed. "That can't be."

"That's what the name says. We told the lottery director Leo Kellogg's name, maybe she figures this has something to do with our lost man."

"But Sara got that check for all that money. Why, and how, would she have the winning ticket?"

Doyle walked to his desk, followed by Oscar. "Maybe that check came from the lottery winnings, to throw us off. Maybe she didn't think that the lottery people would let us know. We never told Sara that we went there, did we?"

"I don't remember mentioning it to her. I never talk about our findings until we get everything together. She couldn't have known we had the winner's list."

"So, did she get the ticket from dear old dad, or did she do him in to get it?" Doyle pondered out loud.

"Damn, and she seemed like such a nice person."

"Let's not jump to conclusions yet. We need to talk to her. Do you remember where you dropped her off at?" Doyle asked.

"Yeah, not too far from here."

Doyle's Law

"Okay, let's go find out what the hell is going on." Doyle called over to Marge, still knitting and listening to music. She was in her own little world. "Marge," he said. She jumped and looked to Doyle. "We're going back out. You know the drill."

"Should I lock up if you don't get back before closing?" she asked.

Doyle looked at his watch, it was almost three now. "Sure, turn off the lights and lock up. See you in the morning if we don't get back before closing."

She waved them off and went back to her knitting, listening to Bob Seger singing "*Turn the Page*."

He led Oscar out to the car. "Too bad we can't park the car on the sidewalk in front of the office. Save us from having to walk around to the back," Oscar said.

Doyle stopped and thought. "You know, there's a door at the back of the office behind a pile of plywood leaning against the wall. I'll bet if we move the plywood it will go out to the back."

Oscar stared, "Now you think of this. I wonder about you."

"Get in the car, besides, you need the exercise walking around the building." Doyle smiled. "Navigate me to Sara's place."

They drove out and Oscar told Doyle where to go. They got to a small house on a street with a few boarded up homes. There were a couple burned out buildings, also. A sad statement on Detroit's condition, Doyle thought. Oscar pointed to a house and said, "That's it."

They got out and went to the building. Doyle was going to knock, but saw a note taped to the door. He looked closer at the small handwriting and read aloud, "*Have gone out of town. May be back in a few days. Sara.*"

"Well, this is just fine," Oscar said. "She evidently isn't worried about whether we find her father or not. There's no phone number or a place to reach her?"

"Nothing," Doyle said. "No phone, no contact. She's in the wind. Now I'm getting suspicious."

"You think she was in on this? Maybe she and her father are pulling a scam? Is the ticket they have even theirs?" Oscar said.

"They could have found someone with the winning ticket and took it from them. It's a thought," Doyle said.

"Yeah, our mystery person in Sterling Heights. He could have been the ticket owner," Oscar said.

"That's my thought now, too. And since Sara is being very mysterious about this, I'm suspecting that's what's going on."

"But why come to us?" Oscar said. "They should have known we would investigate and maybe find out their plot?"

Doyle was silent, thinking. "It doesn't make sense, does it? Why bring us in on it?"

"Now we have to find the Sterling Heights person and Sara. Besides her father," Oscar said. "This is getting complicated."

Doyle thought there was no way to find her for now. "Maybe we should just write this off."

"Hey, we saw two deaths because of this. Besides, our pride is at stake," Oscar said.

Doyle looked at him and smiled. Oscar was an optimist. Doyle saw the bad side of things. Doyle didn't really know Oscar all that well. They had worked in the same squad, but were never teamed together. But, he knew Oscar was a very good cop and had a high rate of solving cases. That's why he asked Oscar to join him.

"You're right as always. So, what shall we do now, Dr. Watson?"

Oscar laughed and replied, "Shall we rest our minds for the day, Holmes?"

"Sounds good, you head home and I'll go back and send Marge home, too. I have some phone calls to make."

They went to the car and drove back. Doyle dropped Oscar at his car and parked. Doyle waved to Oscar as he drove by and away. Doyle looked at the door in the back of the building. It was boarded up. He'd have to pull the boards off and see what was under it. Hopefully a good door. He walked around the building, went in and got a surprise. Val was standing at Marge's desk talking.

He went to them and gave Val a quick kiss. "What are you two plotting?"

Marge smiled and said, "You have a delightful lady friend here, Arthur. We were just talking about you behind your back."

"I was wondering why my ears were burning. What are you doing here, and how did you find me?"

"That's no way to greet me. You should ask how my day is going and tell me that you're glad to see me."

"Okay, sorry, I'm glad to see you and how's your day going?" he asked.

"Shall we go to your desk and sit. I have good news to tell you."

Doyle looked at Marge. "Go home, I'll close up. I don't think we'll have any more clients coming in."

Marge gathered her things and stood. "I'll see you bright and early in the morning. Nice to meet you, Val, don't keep him up too late." She grinned and winked, then went out.

"She's quite nice. Your grandmother?"

"Heaven's no. But, she would be a nice grandmother. Now, come and sit and tell me your good news."

They went to Doyle's desk. She looked at the messy desk covered in papers and empty styrofoam cups, then said, "Love what you've done with the place."

"Well, it's me. You haven't seen my apartment yet. You may not want to know me after that." He sat and motioned her to the chair next to his desk. She sat. "So, what's the good news?"

"I quit my job," she said. "Now I can see you more often."

"That is good news, but how will you live without an income?" he asked, hoping she wasn't going to live off of him. Not that he would mind, but his income wasn't the best right now.

Doyle's Law

"That's the second part of the good news. I was divorced from Ken, but his life insurance policy still listed me as beneficiary. And since he didn't die of natural causes, it may be covered under double indemnity. As soon as the insurance company decides, they will issue me the check. I'll have a good amount of money to live on."

That relieved Doyle from having to support her. He never thought about a life insurance policy. "Did Ken have a pension from the police force? He may have been let go, but he could have had money in a fund."

She paused, thinking. "I don't know, but I'll call HR at his precinct and see. It's worth a look."

She stood and went to him, sitting on his lap. She gave him a nice long kiss and then whispered in his ear. "Why don't you lock the door and we can fool around in the office. Maybe the boss won't find out."

Doyle laughed and said, "I think he already knows. But, he'll look away."

He went and locked the front door, putting the sign in the window saying they would be open at eight in the morning. He went back to her. "Only problem is, there's no place to enjoy a roll in the hay. The only couch is in the front window where everyone can see, and there are no mattresses in the back."

"Okay, then we will go back to my place, or yours." She smiled.

"Let's go to mine. I can change my clothes for work in the morning. Is your car in the back?"

"Yes."

"I'll drive you back in the morning and you can meet Oscar, my partner. He's been dying to see what you look like. I told him you were a goddess, and he's anxiously wanting to meet you."

"A goddess? That just earned you points."

"Shall we go before we lose the mood?"

Forty minutes later, they arrived at Doyle's apartment and went to the door. "I told you I'm not the neatest person, and my maid isn't due until…well, never. So, don't expect much."

He opened the door and they went in. She found it to look like most bachelor's apartments, not that she had been in that many. "Okay, it just needs a woman's touch."

"Or a bulldozer." Doyle went to the kitchen to check his answering machine.

"You still use an answering machine? What about voicemail?"

"I don't trust voicemail, it's stored on some system somewhere, and the NSA could tap into it. Here I have the message on my machine and can erase it anytime."

"That's very true. Now I can call you and leave dirty talk, right?"

"I'll expect it." He grinned and pulled her to him.

*

Chapter 20

Doyle was awakened by a banging noise. He looked around and found he was in bed. He heard the noise again and reached for his Sig on the nightstand. He looked over and saw that Val wasn't with him. The noise continued and he got out of bed, pulled his jogging pants on, and went to the door, opened it and went out.

He walked quietly down the hall to investigate. When he got to the living room, he was shocked by what he saw - his living room was clean. Other than a pile of laundry in the middle of the floor, it was spotless. The end tables were devoid of plates and beer bottles. The couch had the pillows straightened and there were flowers in a vase on the TV.

He let out a quiet groan and went to the kitchen to find out what the banging was. He looked around the corner and found Val, wearing one of his shirts, trying to break out the ice in the freezer with a kitchen knife.

"You'll be at it all day," he said, causing her to jump.

"Don't do that. Make some noise before you enter a room."

"And have you throw a chunk of ice at me? No thank you." He went to her and put his arms around her from the back as she kept whacking away at the ice.

"Don't you ever defrost this thing?" she asked.

"Why? I never use it," he replied.

"I know, I found boxes of food that expired over a year ago. Do you eat out a lot?"

"Every chance I get. Can you cook?"

"I eat out a lot, too," she said.

Doyle looked at his watch and said, "I have to be at work in three hours, did you get any sleep?"

"I passed out just before you rolled off me," she laughed.

"Funny. I'm going back to bed. You can go back to chopping ice. Quietly, please." He kissed her and went back to the bedroom.

Seven-forty five, Doyle and Val were at the office. Marge and Oscar were at their desks and Oscar's eyes grew when he saw Val. Doyle brought her to Oscar and smiled.

"Oscar, this is Val. Val this is the infamous Oscar Drew."

Oscar jumped up and came around his desk. Val grabbed onto him with a hug. He had a surprised look and smiled widely. "Nice to meet you, Val," he said. "My pleasure. Happy to meet you."

"Oscar, you're starting to babble," Doyle said.

Val let him go and he said, "Sorry, I'm just surprised."

"Surprised?" Val said.

"I didn't think Art actually had a lady friend. You are a pleasure to see, I mean meet."

"Pull your tongue back in. Anything on Sara yet?"

"I made a number of calls, she either drove out on her own or had someone drive her. She took nothing in public transportation."

"Well, keep at it. I'll be in my office." He grinned and took Val to his desk.

Oscar called over, "We need walls."

"Yeah, yeah. I'll work on it," Doyle replied.

"And a mattress in the back," Val whispered.

"You can go home now, I have work to do," he told her.

She kissed him and went to Marge. They talked a bit then Val left.

Oscar came running over. "I really didn't believe you about how good looking she is. Wow. Does she have a sister?"

"Don't know, never asked her," Doyle said.

"But you will, right?"

Doyle laughed and said, "I'll see what I can do. Now, we have a case to investigate. I was thinking we need to talk to Sara's neighbors. They may know something that can help."

"Good idea, I should have thought of that. Anytime you want to go, I'm ready."

Doyle was thinking, "Where would I order cubicle walls?"

"That was a quick change of conversation. I don't know, but I can look them up online. I'll Google them on my laptop." He turned and went back to his desk.

Bob Moats

Doyle started to open the mail that Marge must have picked up when she came in. He liked that they delivered early. One letter had hand writing on it and no stamp, he opened that first. It had no return address, which always made him curious. He took the folded sheet of paper out and found a money order for five hundred dollars wrapped in it. He started to read the letter that was written in crude handwriting. It reminded him of someone who was writing on some surface that wasn't meant for writing. He read and then called Oscar.

"What is it?" Oscar asked, going over to Doyle's desk.

"This was in with the mail, it has no return address, and no stamp for that matter. Must have been dropped through the mail chute before the mail came. He handed it to Oscar and he read aloud.

"Dear Mr. Doyle and Mr. Drew, thank you for everything you attempted to do to find my father. He has returned and I'm happy for it. Please accept this money order for payment for your time. I'll no longer be needing your services, thank you again, Sara Kellogg."

Oscar looked at Doyle, "This is very strange. To have written this out and not come in to tell us. And to have mysteriously disappeared from her home. Sounds to me like she's trying to get rid of us. I smell something rotten."

"I'm thinking the same." Doyle put the money order in his desk drawer and stood. "Let's go back to her house and talk to the neighbors."

"What about the walls?"

"Later, they'll wait. We need to find Sara Kellogg, now."

"Great, now we're after both of them. A double header," Oscar said and followed Doyle to the door.

Doyle turned to Marge, sitting knitting. "We'll be back, take any messages."

She smiled and said she would. The men went back out and around the building.

"Did you ever look at that back door you said was there?" Oscar asked.

"Suck it up and walk. You need to lose some weight," Doyle said with a subtle grin.

"So that means you haven't looked yet. Hey, I'm not overweight. I'm a little paunchy, but it's all muscle."

"The only muscles are in your head," Doyle said as they reached the car. Doyle drove out and over to Sara's house. They parked out front and got out, going back up to the house.

Doyle told Oscar, "Look through the windows on that side of the house to see what you can see."

Oscar went around the building while Doyle went the other way. He was looking through a window into what must be a bedroom. He saw women's lingerie on a chair and figured it must be Sara's room. He went to the next window and had to bend down as the shade was pulled down, but not all the way. He could see a bed that looked like it hadn't been slept on in a while. It was still made up. He glanced around the room and saw men's clothing on a rack.

He heard a noise to his left and turned to see an older man with a shotgun aimed at him. He stood up and said, "Take it easy, man. I'm not doing anything wrong."

"Sticking your nose into that house is wrong. You don't live there, so what are you doing?" He brought the gun up to aim at Doyle's head.

"As I said, take it easy. That thing could go off."

"Damn right it could. Blow your fool head off, it will," the man threatened.

Doyle didn't look directly at Oscar coming around the other side of the man. He didn't want the man to see him looking at Oscar.

"Talk or I'll Swiss cheese you," the man demanded.

Oscar snuck up quietly behind him and reached around, grabbing the shotgun and pulled it up. The man had squeezed the trigger, blasting up into the air. Doyle jumped to the man and pulled the gun from his hands.

"What the hell do you think you're doing?" Doyle yelled at the man. "You could kill someone with this thing."

"What the hell do you think you're doing peeking into their house? You some kinda peeping tom?"

"I'm a private investigator hired by Sara Kellogg to find her father, that's what I'm doing peeping into the house. Sara is missing now, and we're trying to find her."

The man stood quietly and said, "Sara is missing? I knew her father had taken off, but I hadn't heard Sara was gone. When?"

Doyle handed the shotgun to Oscar who unloaded it. Then he handed it back to the man.

"As far as we know, she's been missing since late yesterday. She left a note at my office stating her father came back. You haven't seen him around have you?"

"No, I haven't. He was a mean man, always yelling and complaining about everything. I don't know how Sara put up with him. I haven't seen him around since last week. What's he done now?"

"What do you mean?"

"Well, he was busting up some boxes in the back and then he was acting real strange. I saw him talking to some man in the back and that man looked shady."

"Can you describe him?"

The old man told Doyle what he saw and when he finished, Doyle grinned.

"Did I say something funny?" the man asked.

"No, you described a man I had met the other day. He wasn't a nice man to have around." He turned to Oscar and said, "Our friend here just described Louis, my favorite bookie."

*

Chapter 21

"If you're going back to that pool hall to talk to him, I'm going with you," Oscar said. "Maybe I'll meet a hot waitress."

Doyle ignored him and asked the old man, "Did you hear what they were saying?"

He stood a moment, looking like he was thinking, then said, "Well, they were sorta arguing. I heard money mentioned a couple times, but Leo was always into someone for money. He had no luck with betting or money. Poor Sara, she always ended up bailing him out."

"Did she have the money to bail him out?" Doyle asked.

"I don't know where she got it from, but I heard her yelling at him about how she always had to pay for his gambling. She must have had some money stashed away."

"Good to know," Doyle said and turned to Oscar. "Well, you'll get your chance to go look at waitresses. Thank you, sir, for your help." Doyle took out a card and handed it to the old man. "If you should see either Sara or her father, call me right away."

The man looked at the card and said he would. "Do I get a reward if I call?"

139

Doyle frowned, thinking that everyone wants something, instead of just helping. "I guess I can see that you'll get something."

"How much?"

"Don't push it, just be happy you helped Sara." Doyle turned and went out to the car followed by Oscar.

"So, you told me that Louis said he hadn't seen Leo, but now we find out he had, and recently. Could Louis have had anything to do with Leo's disappearance?" Oscar wondered.

"Maybe Leo is hiding out from Louis, but what about Sara turning in the winning ticket? Did Leo know about that? Maybe he told Sara to turn the ticket in for him so he wasn't implicated in the two murders, or keeping Louis from finding out he had money. Nice father."

Doyle's cell phone rang and he looked at the caller ID, it said private. He hated those, but answered, "Doyle here."

"Art, It's Harry Lowe. I did some checking and found your last local winner on the list. The one in Mt. Clemens. The sheriffs tracked him down to see if he was all right. He wasn't. They found him passed out and dying. They got him to the hospital, but he expired shortly after. Medical Examiner said he was poisoned. Slow acting, but deadly. You got three dead winners."

"Can you call the police up in Traverse City and over to Grand Rapids? Have them check on the last two people on the list," Doyle asked.

"I already did, they said they'd track them down and get back to me. I'll let you know."

"Thanks, Harry. Talk later." Doyle clicked off and looked at Oscar.

"Another death?" Oscar asked.

"Yeah, this is getting serious. I don't understand how Leo or Sara could think they'd get away with killing off the other winners. Doesn't make sense."

"Or, they are both too stupid to realize the implications of what they're doing," Oscar said.

"That's true. You still need to get that envelope in to forensics to see if they can get any prints. You have a friend in the lab, I hope?"

"I got friends all over the place. Comes from being a loveable kind of guy," Oscar said.

"No comment," Doyle said and started the car. He drove over to their office and dropped Oscar off at his car. "If you get any results, call me. Oh, and if you see Cadeem, kick him in the balls for me."

Oscar laughed and got out, went to his car and drove off. Doyle went back in the office and found Marge relaxing.

"Done knitting?" he asked.

"Just relaxing my hands, damn arthritis is getting worse," she said.

"Sorry to hear that. Any messages?"

"Nope, I hope you get more business than this," she said.

Doyle laughed. "Getting bored already?"

"I understand that it's going to be slow at first, but I'll survive. I'd just like to see you do well. How's your case going?"

"Don't ask, I'm not getting any good vibes from this. We need a decent break in the case."

Doyle went to his desk and sat. He thought about calling Val to see how she as doing, then he decided to wait until later.

About an hour later, his cell phone played *Jaws* and he looked at the caller ID. It was Oscar. "Anything yet?"

"Amazingly, yes. I had a friend do a test on the envelope and he got a couple sets of prints. Small ones, which probably were Sara's, and those weren't in the database. Two other partials came up fairly quickly. Both were Leo's. Got a hit from the criminal database, and since he was in the prison system, they came in fast."

"So, Sara got the money from Leo. Did she know, or was she telling us the truth that she found the money at the door? Come back in, we need to go to the pool hall and find Louis."

"About time. I'll be right there." Oscar hung up.

Shortly after, they were heading back to the pool hall where Doyle met Val. Since she quit, he knew she wouldn't be there.

"I hope you're not setting yourself up for a letdown trying to find a hot waitress," Doyle said to Oscar.

"I've had so many disappointments in my life, it wouldn't surprise me. Now, what are we going to do if Louis is here?"

"I'm thinking plan B," Doyle said with a grin.

"Works for me, but no bandage wraps. Want me to stay in the background to watch your back?"

Doyle thought on that, especially since he was attacked by the big thug. "That works for me. Stay close but keep an eye out for fast moving bruisers. You're armed, aren't you?"

"I wouldn't leave home without it."

Doyle pulled into the parking lot. There were about as many cars as last time, so Doyle hoped Louis was in there collecting. They went in the front door and stood looking around the room. Oscar never saw Louis, but Doyle described him. How many men wore sharkskin jackets with bolo ties?

They walked around the room, everyone was silent while a player lined up a shot, then they all cheered as the balls dropped into the pockets. Doyle stopped and tapped Oscar, pointing to a man talking to two others.

"It's him. Let's go behind him and see what he's up to."

They walked around the outer perimeter of the crowd and came up behind Louis. Doyle looked around to see if Louis' bodyguard was around. He saw the hulk standing a ways from Louis, leaning against the wall. Doyle pointed out the big man to Oscar and said to keep an eye on him.

The two men talking to Louis hurried off after handing him some cash, probably for a bet. Doyle told Oscar to stay where he was and watch the hulk. Doyle walked up behind Louis and drew his Sig. He leaned in and whispered into Louis' ear, "We meet again, Louie. You know the drill." Then he poked the gun into the man's back.

Louis stiffened and said, "Crap, not again." Then he turned and went to the back door.

They were out in the alley again and Doyle roughly grabbed Louis by the back collar and pulled him around to face him.

"You lied to me, Louie. You said you hadn't seen Leo, but I got word from a nosy neighbor that you visited him last week. Why'd you lie to me?"

Louis was glancing at the back door and looking nervous. "I forgot. That's all."

Louis smiled as the back door opened, but looked shocked when his goon came flying out face first onto the ground. Oscar was behind him at the door, pointing his .38 at the goon and smiling.

"Louie, meet my partner Oscar. He doesn't like enforcers for low life bookies. Now, talk to me about seeing Leo. And don't B.S. me."

The man on the ground turned over and saw Oscar standing over him with the gun aimed at his legs. The color drained from his face and he curled up into a fetal position. Louis was watching the big man hoping he'd do something, but saw he was on his own.

"Okay, I told a little fib. I did see Leo last week, just to collect what he owed me, that's all."

"Now, talk about how Leo's daughter was taking care of his debts. Where did she get the money?"

"Money? She didn't have any money," Louis replied.

"The neighbor told me that Sara was mad because she had to take care of Leo's debts. Are you saying he was a liar?"

144

"I ain't saying that, Leo's daughter didn't have any money. So I took it out in trade. If you know what I mean."

Doyle realized what Louis meant and felt nauseated at the thought of this creep man-handling Sara. He stared at the greasy little man and then threw him into the side of the dumpster. It rang out with a loud clanging thud and Louis collapsed to the ground.

"Did he say what I think he said?" Oscar asked.

"I do believe so," Doyle spat and went to pull Louis from the ground. He pushed his forearm into Louis' throat, pinning him against the dumpster. Louis' eyes were bugging out and his face contorted in fear.

"Hey, man. You're hurting me," he whined.

"I'll do worse than that if you did what I think you did," Doyle growled.

"Hey, the old man didn't have the cash so I made a deal to take it out on his daughter. She agreed so I wouldn't have to put the hurt on him. She was good, too."

Doyle was trying to contain his rage, but failed. He pulled Louis away from the dumpster and flung him to the ground. He started kicking Louis relentlessly. Oscar rushed up behind Doyle and said, "Careful, Art. Don't leave bruises."

*

Chapter 22

Doyle pulled Louis up from the ground and stood him up against the dumpster. "You ever touch Sara again, I swear I'll bust every bone in your slimly body. I'll start with that bone between your legs. Got it asshole?"

Louis nodded his head quickly, not speaking. He was suffering from his beating and didn't want another go around. Doyle got his face real close to Louis and said, "I mean it." Louis bit his lip and said nothing.

Doyle pulled Louis away from the dumpster and dropped him on the goon, still on the ground. They both just laid there, not moving. Doyle stood, giving them both a stare that said he wasn't happy. "Another thing, Louie, you will forget every bet owed to you by Leo. Any questions?" Louis nodded his head. Doyle gave him an extra kick, then he turned to Oscar.

"We have to find Sara and Leo. Let's get out of here, the stench is getting bad back here." They went back through the door and out the front to their car.

"Were you able to spot a hot waitress?" Doyle asked as they got to the car.

"I looked around while watching the hulk. There were two, but they were lukewarm. You got the last good hot one."

"Sorry," Doyle said and started the car. "I'm heading back to Sara's house. We need to get inside and see what we can find."

"That would work, maybe. You think we may find a body or two in the house?" Oscar said with a grin.

"That's not funny. I hope we don't find a body." Doyle pulled out and headed back to Sara's. "Speaking of bodies, I was thinking, don't the heirs of the dead winners have a right to the winnings?"

"I hadn't thought of that. I would imagine that it would depend on the lottery people. I think they have some provisions about that. The money may not go anywhere if the winner hadn't signed the paperwork yet. Besides, they haven't doled out any money yet, which makes me wonder how Leo afforded the check Sara got from dear old dad."

"Now that the sixth winner has appeared, they should begin the check awarding. Even if they are short three people. The winners from Traverse City and Grand Rapids would have to come in to get their winnings," Doyle said.

"For the big win, they don't collect the money in Detroit, they have to go to Lansing to get it," Oscar said.

"You're just a fountain of information about the lottery," Doyle said with a grin. "Wait, you say they have to go to Lansing?"

"Yep, the main lottery headquarters is in the capital of Michigan."

"So, if Leo or Sara went out of town, maybe they went to Lansing?" Doyle was thinking.

"That's very possible. They usually like to have the winners together to take pictures."

"The logistics of that would be difficult. But I guess if I was getting millions of dollars, I'd take the time to be there when they tell me. Shall we find out when the winners are getting their checks?"

"I'm on top of that," Oscar said, pulling his phone. "I still have the lottery number from when I called the other day." He dialed and then listened. He talked to someone on the other end, explaining that he wanted to know when the ceremony was for the cash give away for the Mega Millions. He listened and then hung up. "Tomorrow at one. It's a ninety minute drive there, want to go tonight and stay over?"

"No, we can drive up in the morning. We'll get there in plenty of time. I don't like motels."

"No? Why not?" Oscar asked.

"I just don't, so don't ask."

Oscar knew better than to push, so he sat back and watched the scenery. They got to Sara's house and parked. "Shall we go find the old man before he shoots us?" Oscar asked as they walked up to the house.

"That may be a good idea. Go bang on his door and warn him we're here."

Before Oscar could go, the old man came around the back of his house between the houses. "You two back again. I didn't call."

"We know, we're needing to get into the house to see if there was any foul play, maybe we'll find a body," Doyle said, hoping to get the man interested in helping them.

"A body? Now that's interesting, can I come along?" he said.

Doyle smiled and said, "You sure can. Do you know the best way into the house?"

"The back door is messed up, doesn't lock too well. You can push it and it will open."

"Good, lead us there," Doyle said.

They walked around the back and up to the door. It was old and the paint was peeling off in long strips. Doyle reached up and shook the knob, it was loose. He gave the door a shove and it did open easily. The old man smiled and said, "Told ya."

Doyle yelled into the house, "Hello, anyone in there?" He listened and yelled again. No answer came from the house. He moved carefully into the kitchen just off the back door. It smelled like spoiled food, but no smell of decomp from a rotting body. The men stood in the kitchen looking around. Nothing popped out as evidence in any crime.

They went out of the kitchen and into a dining room. There was a large oval dining table with six chairs around it. There were papers and books all over the table. Doyle lifted one and looked at the title. "*Poisons and Antidotes of the World,*" he read aloud.

"Well, this would be an answer for the murdered man in Mt. Clemens. He was poisoned." Doyle opened the book to the front flap and found it was on loan from the Masonic library. "That explains Leo's visit to the library. He set the book back down and followed Oscar and the old man into a living room.

It was an old fashioned room, all decorated in knick-knacks on small wooden shelves. The furniture looked like thrift shop chic and the wood floor was partially covered by a round oriental rug. It didn't fit in with the rest of the decor, but it was functional. Doyle checked the tables, only finding ash trays filled with cigarette butts.

Doyle turned to the old man, "Did Leo or Sara smoke?"

"Leo, he smoked like a coal fire in a furnace."

Doyle chuckled at the reference. He went to a hallway and up to the first door. It was a bedroom, the one he saw earlier through the window. It was Sara's.

He looked over the top of the dresser at all the objects scattered around. He found various women things - make-up, perfumes and hair stuff. There were photos of Sara and her father. He found one with her father and a woman. He figured it was her mother. He went to the closet and opened it. There was a suitcase on the floor, so Doyle figured she wasn't taking a long trip.

Oscar came in and said, "I checked the next bedroom. It had to be Leo's and it hasn't been used in a while. Bed is still made and the closet had lots of clothes. He had a low dresser and I found a letter from someone asking about a price for the ticket. No return name. Sounds like someone was buying his winnings, but why would he sell?"

"Quick money, no questions asked about where Leo got the ticket. Leo probably stole it or murdered someone for it. But was afraid that he'd be found with it. Someone paid him less than it was worth, but enough to keep him happy," Doyle said.

"So why are they going to collect on the ticket?" Oscar asked.

The old man came in and said, "While you two were rummaging, I did some investigating. I found this. 'X' marks the spot," he handed a map to Doyle.

Doyle smiled as he looked at the name on the map, Lansing. "They forgot to take it with them," Doyle said. He opened the map and the old man came up and pointed to an 'X' over what Doyle figured to be the lottery office. "Thank you…I don't even know your name."

"Joseph James, but everyone calls me Jesse James. I was a criminal at one time. I robbed banks back when they were easy to rob. Did my time and was paroled two years ago, too much crowding in the prison. Damn criminals nowadays."

Doyle laughed and then took the map and put it in his jacket pocket. "We may need this tomorrow." He looked at Jesse James and asked, "Is there a basement?"

"Sure is, all these houses have basements. I'll show you where." He turned back to the kitchen and showed them a door on the side. Doyle thanked him and went to the door. It was dark at the bottom,

Doyle found a light switch and flipped it. There was now light at the bottom of the stairs.

"Anyone afraid to go into the basement?" Doyle asked, then laughed evilly. He went down as Oscar followed behind with his .38 in hand.

Jesse said to Oscar, "That's a nice gun you got there."

"Thanks, I like it," Oscar replied.

Doyle reached the bottom and looked around. There was a dirt floor and concrete block walls. There were shelves containing various boxes and bags that looked like they had been there a long while. Doyle walked to the end of a row of shelves and stopped. He pointed to what he found on the ground.

A dead body.

*

Chapter 23

"I was just kidding about finding a body," Oscar said.

Doyle went to the corpse wrapped in plastic and studied the man. He cut open the plastic with his knife and saw the markings of a severe blow to the head, but looking around, he saw no blood in the area. "He wasn't murdered here, just hidden from view."

"I've never seen him before. Who is he?" the old man asked.

Doyle went through his pockets and pulled out a wallet. He went through it and said, "Daniel Wasserman." He looked to Oscar and said, "His address is in Sterling Heights. I think we found our mystery man."

"Do you think he was killed by Leo or Sara?" Oscar asked.

"I hope not Sara," Doyle said. "I don't know Leo that well, but I think he would do this out of desperation. I think Daniel here offered them money for the ticket, but Leo decided to keep the money and the ticket. Daniel didn't like being stiffed, so Leo made him a stiff."

"Should we call the police?" Oscar asked.

"We should, but if we do, then both Sara and Leo will be arrested. You know very well how the judicial system works. Guilty before proven innocent. We need to get to them and get this figured out. I don't want the wrong person to end up being convicted unfairly."

"So, we just leave him here?" Oscar asked as Doyle looked to the old man.

"Jesse, as a former criminal, would you be opposed to a little larceny?" Doyle asked.

"You want to move the body, is that what you're thinking?" Jesse asked, smiling.

"Well, we can't leave him down here to decay. We can put him in the park down around the corner.

Doyle's Law

Then, Jesse, you can call the police and let them know you were walking by and found the body."

"How are we going to take him out of here without raising suspicion?" Jesse asked.

"Have you ever seen 'Weekend at Bernie's'?" Doyle smiled. "Oscar, grab that hat on the shelf and cover his wound, then take him under his right arm."

They carried the body up the stairs and into the kitchen. Doyle said to stop, "I think it would be easier to put him on the back porch of the boarded house next door. They all agreed and went out the back door, Oscar and Doyle carrying the body between them.

Jesse was leading the way to give them a little credibility. Luckily there was no one in the backyards of the half-deserted neighborhood. Unless there were people in the boarded up buildings or burned out homes, they wouldn't be seen. They decided to take him a couple houses down and set him on the back porch. Doyle wiped down the wallet and put it back in his pocket.

"At least they'll be able to identify the body and notify any next of kin," he said. "Let's get out of here before we're seen."

They went back to Sara's house and stood in the kitchen. "Jesse, give us a while before you call the police," Doyle said. "Oscar and I are going to Lansing to where we believe Sara and Leo should be. Hopefully we can get this settled. Thanks for your help, Jesse."

"It's on me, no charge. Let's just say it was fun to do something illegal again," the old man said with a grin.

"Just remember, you helped move the body, so that incriminates you too," Oscar said.

"Good friends help you move, really good friends help you move a body," Jesse said. "I heard that on *CSI* one night."

"Very true, now we'll get out of here, we have some traveling to do. Let's go, Oscar."

They closed the back door and went out to the car. Doyle looked back and saw Jesse standing between the houses waving to them. Doyle was starting to like the old man.

"Now where to?" Oscar asked as they pulled away from the house.

"Back to the office, and then home to get ready for our long drive in the morning."

"Are you going to see your hot waitress tonight?"

"I don't know, but probably."

"Ask her if she has a sister."

"I will Oscar, I will."

They arrived back and went in. Marge was knitting and put it down when they came in.

"Anything good on your case yet?" she asked.

Doyle told her about their adventures, but didn't mention finding the body. Something they wouldn't talk about for now.

"Any messages?" Doyle asked.

"Yes, Val called and wanted to talk to you. I told her I'd let you know."

"Thanks," Doyle said and went to his desk.

"I'm going to take a look at that back door," Oscar said. He went back to the pile of plywood standing against the wall and started to move the boards.

He found the door and unhooked the slide bolts securing it closed. He pulled on the door and it gave. It opened inward, but he found the opening was boarded up. He stood there annoyed.

Doyle had dialed Val and she answered. "About time you called."

"I've been busy moving bodies," Doyle joked. "That's not for publication, it's an inside joke. What's up, Marge said you called."

"Just wanted to know if you were coming by tonight. I want to take you to dinner, on me. I got a check today from the insurance company. I'm a rich woman now."

"Great, but I won't marry you for your money."

"Would you marry me for my body?" she said with a laugh.

"Maybe, but I'm not into marriage for now. I can come by, but it will have to be a short night, Oscar and I are going to Lansing tomorrow to track down our client and her missing father."

"Okay, so I'll get you to bed early."

"Better still, come to my house. That way I can leave early and get back here without rushing. You can go home at your leisure."

"Works for me. See you later." She hung up and Doyle turned to see what the noise was coming from the back of the building. He stood and went to Oscar pounding on the boards covering the door opening.

"Don't hurt your fists. You need a sledge hammer to break through that," Doyle said to Oscar as the man kept pounding.

Oscar stopped and said, "You got some kind of fancy gung-fooey skills. Use your kicks to knock the boards out."

"Better yet," Doyle said and went to the tools they'd left from the work they did getting the building ready, and picked up a crowbar. He went to the doorway and stuck the bar into the frame and started pulling. Slowly, the nails in the boards started to give way and finally the men were able to push them the rest of the way out. They stood looking out at the back parking lot.

"Now, that's better. We don't have to walk around the building," Oscar said, as they walked outside.

"You'll get fat and lazy," Doyle said and went back into the building. He closed the door on Oscar and locked it. He could hear Oscar protesting outside. "Walk around," Doyle yelled at the door. Now he could hear Oscar swearing. He looked at the door, it had no key lock, it was missing from the hole, so they would have to mount a deadbolt on the door.

Doyle went back to his desk as Oscar came storming in. "I did all the work to start getting the door opened and you lock me out."

"It needs a deadbolt and key, otherwise we can't get in from the outside."

"Fine," Oscar said, still sounding mad. "I'll go to the hardware store and get one. Maybe I'll walk into a robbery and be a big hero, too." He went to the back door and unlocked it, going out after slamming the door.

"I'd say he was a little annoyed," Marge said, watching the whole incident.

"He's lucky I didn't lock the front door, too," Doyle laughed.

"Do you think you'll find Sara and her father?"

"I think we're getting closer. All the signs are pointing to our finding them tomorrow in Lansing."

"Do you think you'll get paid after all this work?" she asked.

Doyle suddenly remembered the money order in his drawer. He opened the drawer and took the check out. He stood and went to Marge. "We already got paid, I forgot about this." He handed the check to Marge and told her to deposit it in the bank. She looked at it and asked "Where do you bank?"

"Oh, that's right. I haven't got you set up with that, seeing as we haven't had any income yet." He went to his desk and took out the bank book and gave it to her. "May as well hang on to this since you'll be doing the deposits. The bank is around the corner, Comerica. Just fill out the deposit slip using the numbers from the book and deposit it."

"I can do that," she replied.

"It's getting late, and I don't see anyone coming in, so go deposit that and head home. We'll be in early to go to Lansing, so maybe I'll see you then."

"You got it, see you in the morning, maybe." She gathered her purse and knitting bag and went out.

Doyle watched her go and thought that he should have let her out the back door. He figured they would get used to it eventually. He went back to his desk and sat waiting for Oscar to return.

*

Chapter 24

Doyle closed up making sure the backdoor was locked. Oscar hadn't returned yet, but he had a key to get back into the building. Doyle drove back to his apartment thinking about tomorrow. Would they find Sara or Leo? Would they solve the mystery of all the murdered winners and losers? He wondered if Jesse called the police and if so, what did they do about the body? He was sure he'd find out eventually.

Doyle pulled into his parking lot and saw Val sitting on the trunk of her car. He parked and went to her.

"I'm sorry to make you wait," he said.

"I've only been here a few minutes. I've been keeping busy deciding how I'm going to spend my money."

"And what did you come up with?"

"All kinds of nice things."

"Anything for me?"

"You have me, so you don't need anything else."

"True, let's go in."

Doyle got ready to go out to dinner. He had to dress nicely since Val had a dress on. He came out of the bedroom and she approved of his attire, commenting on how well he cleaned up, and they went out to the car.

On the way to the restaurant Val asked, "How's your case going? Have you found the father yet?"

"We hope to find them tomorrow in Lansing," Doyle replied.

"What's up there?"

"The lottery headquarters. Sara turned up having the winning ticket and she has to be there tomorrow for the ceremony to get her check and have pictures taken."

"Sounds pompous," she said with a grin.

"The state needs to show ordinary people getting rich, so others will drop their paychecks hoping to cash in. I bought scratch off tickets years ago when the state started this. I continued to buy them hoping to hit it big. In the many years since, I've only won $75, and that was from a ticket the person in line at the store didn't want. I bought it and won. Too bad for that person in front of me. Point is, I have spent tons of money and got nothing much in return."

"Sounds like a scam."

"You've never bought a lottery ticket?" Doyle asked.

"No, I had to save my money for bills and food. A lottery ticket was a luxury, so I never indulged."

"Good for you. Now you can drop thousands of dollars for tickets."

"I still won't buy them," she said, as they arrived at the restaurant.

The dinner went well; they both enjoyed the food and the conversation. Doyle was finding out more about Val, and liking her more. They finished and drove back to Doyle's apartment.

"Do you want a drink?" Doyle asked as he helped her take her jacket off. It was late in September and the weather was getting colder. Doyle wasn't fond of the cold - he tolerated it - so they had to dress warmly.

"Sure, what have you got?" she asked.

He went through the list of drinks he could make and she asked for a beer. Simple enough, he thought.

"Can we just sit and listen to music? I'm tired and want to relax," she asked.

"Sure." He went to his stereo and turned on the FM station that played soft music. He liked to listen to it when he had a stressful day. He gave her the beer and sat next to her with his. They both sat silently on the couch listening to Kenny G playing his music.

After a while, Val kissed him and said she was going to bed. He followed her into the bedroom and they didn't come out until the morning.

Doyle was anxious to get to Lansing, so he gave Val a goodbye kiss and went off. He parked and saw Oscar at the back door working on the lock.

"You didn't make it back last night?" Doyle asked as he came up.

"No, I decided to go home and get some rest. You know us old people, we have to be in bed early. Alone," he mugged.

"I did ask Val if she had a sister, she does."

"Okay, when can I meet her?" Oscar said excitedly.

"In about ten years, she's only eleven years old."

Oscar frowned and said, "I can't win, I'll die alone and they'll find my body being eaten by cats."

"You don't have any cats."

"Then I guess I'll have to start collecting some." He closed the door and tried the key. It unlocked and opened. "There, it's fixed." Oscar stepped into the building and closed the door. Doyle could hear him lock it and yell, "Walk around."

Doyle laughed and went to the front. He entered and found Marge setting up a coffee maker. She smiled and said, "It's too expensive to keep buying coffee from the store around the corner. I had an extra coffee maker and thought I'd bring it in."

"Well, enjoy it. I don't drink coffee, so there's more for you and Oscar." He went to his desk and checked the mail. Nothing of interest. Oscar came up and handed him a key, then went to Marge and gave her one.

"Now we can all come in the back door," he said and turned to Doyle. "Are we ready to travel?"

"I am, are you rested enough for the trip, if not, you can sleep on the back seat."

Oscar smiled and gave him the finger. He went to his desk and picked up a brown paper bag. Doyle saw this and asked, "Are you brown bagging it? Did you pack a lunch for me?"

"I'll share my ham sandwich with you," he said.

"Keep it, let's go." Doyle went to Marge and said, "If it gets too boring, close up and put a sign in the window saying we'll be back tomorrow."

"I'll be alright. I got my knitting and the radio. Now I have coffee, so I'm good to go."

"Okay, we'll see you tomorrow. I doubt we'll be back in the office today, so you're on your own. See you later." He turned and went to the door, followed by Oscar who waved at Marge.

They drove out and over to the I-75 freeway and headed up to Lansing. They would have to take another freeway over to the city and the trip would take about ninety minutes or so, depending on traffic. Oscar sat back and relaxed as Doyle drove.

"If you get tired of driving, I can take over," Oscar offered.

"You won't fall asleep at the wheel, will you?"

"Fine, drive all the way," Oscar said.

They finally arrived in Lansing and Oscar was checking the map taken from Leo's home to navigate to the building they would need. After a half hour of Oscar getting them lost, they finally found the building. There was one parking space across the street from the building and Doyle was heading for it. As he approached another car zipped into the space.

"What the hell. He saw I was going there. Son-of-a-bitch," Doyle exclaimed.

Doyle's Law

Oscar opened his door and said, "I'll take care of this." Oscar went over to the car as the man was opening his door. Oscar pushed the door back and leaned into the man. "Hey bud. You knew we were going for this space. But you wanted to be a dickhead and grab it. My friend and I don't like that."

The man stared at Oscar with an unimpressed look. "What of it?" he said.

Oscar slowly pulled his jacket back showing his .38 in the holster. "My boss is an impatient kinda guy. You know how these *mob* bosses get when they're pissed. Now, why don't you be a good boy and find another space?"

The man's eyes latched onto the gun and he smiled. "Tell your boss I meant no harm, I'll move."

Oscar closed the door and the man drove out quickly. Oscar looked back to Doyle as he pulled into the space. Doyle got out and said, "What did you say to the guy?"

"I reasoned with his better nature - and threatened him," Oscar said with a grin.

"One of these days you'll get us into trouble threatening the wrong guy. But, good work."

They went into the building and were stopped at a check point manned by two guards. Doyle wondered if their weapons were going to be a problem. He showed the first officer his investigators ID and explained their purpose. The guard looked closely at the ID and Doyle told him he was a former Detroit homicide detective now working private. They were tracking a missing man who was a possible murderer.

164

"Murderer? Hope there's no shooting. I'll let you both slide, just don't get in trouble in here," the guard said, and passed them around the metal detector grid.

Doyle asked, "Where are they having the ceremony for the Mega Million winners?"

The man pointed him in the direction and told him where to go. They thanked him and headed off.

"Think we'll find Sara and Leo?" Oscar asked.

"I hope so. At least one of them."

They came to a door that told them they were at the right place. There was a sign on the door saying that all winners should come back at noon. The door was locked.

"Looks like we wait," Doyle said and motioned to a bench on the other side of the hallway. They went and sat. For the next forty minutes they watched people go to the door, read the sign, and walk away.

Doyle was looking down at the cell phone in Oscar's hand. "What are you doing?" he asked.

"There's wi-fi in the building, I'm watching TV until it's time."

Doyle shook his head and said nothing. Oscar was a simple man, he wasn't good looking or macho, but he could take care of himself. Doyle liked the simplicity of the man.

Doyle was scanning the people waiting to get into the office and then turned his attentions down the hall. That's when he saw Sara and her father coming. He nudged Oscar with his elbow and nodded his head towards the approaching pair.

*

Chapter 25

There were three people waiting to get in the office, standing between Doyle and Sara. So she wasn't aware of Doyle and Oscar being there. Doyle waited until they got to the door and read the sign. Doyle stood and went up behind Sara and her father. Oscar stood back waiting to see if either the father or the daughter would run.

"Hello, Sara," Doyle said to her as she looked at the sign on the door.

She jumped upon hearing her name and turned. "Oh my God, Mr. Doyle, what are you doing here?" she said and pointed to her father. "Mr. Doyle, this is my father, I told you that he came back."

"Yes, you did, but from where?"

Sara cleared her throat. Leo just stood there looking shocked. "He was visiting friends and didn't tell me. I had to scold him for it."

"Sara, do you know a man named Daniel Wasserman?" Doyle asked, watching her face. She didn't flinch.

"No, should I?" she asked.

Doyle turned his attentions to her father. "Mr. Kellogg, I'm Art Doyle, private investigator hired by your daughter to find you. Did you know Daniel Wasserman?"

Leo looked away from Doyle, "No, I don't know the man."

"Well, we found his dead body in your basement. Now do you know who he is?"

Leo's eyes grew large and was acting nervous now. Sara said, "Why would there be a dead man in our home? What does that have to with us?"

"Maybe your father can answer that. Right, Leo? We also have three other lottery winners in the Detroit area who turned up dead. One was poisoned and, coincidentally, you have a book on poisons from the Masonic library. What do you know about them?"

Leo started to get edgy, shifting from side to side and fidgeting with his hands. Doyle figured he was getting ready to run. He glanced back at Oscar and nodded. Doyle said, "Mr. Kellogg, did you murder four people, all for a lottery ticket?"

Leo suddenly pushed Doyle with both hands, causing him to fall back. Doyle was surprised at how strong Leo was. Leo took off as Doyle yelled to Oscar, "Stop him!"

Doyle jumped up and pursued, watching as Leo collided with Oscar, shoving him down with both hands as he passed, and kept moving. Doyle yelled to Oscar, "Stay with Sara." He followed Leo down the hall heading back toward the main entrance.

The two of them ran along the hall, Leo trying to find his way out. He turned a corner and saw the entrance, and sprinted towards it. Doyle skidded around the corner and saw the guard they met when they came in. He yelled, "Stop him, he's the murderer!"

The guard, taken by surprise, turned, but had no time to respond as Leo ran up behind the second guard and grabbed him. Leo spun the man around, using him as a human shield, and snatched the man's gun from its holster. Leo put the gun to the man's head and yelled for everyone to back off.

Both Doyle and the first guard had their guns trained on Leo, but didn't shoot They didn't want to harm the other guard. Doyle aimed his weapon at Leo's head, but had a sudden flashback to the day with Crazy Joe and the mayor. He found himself filled with doubts about firing at Leo. What if he screwed up and hit the guard? Damn it, he thought, now was not the time to lose his nerve, an innocent man's life was on the line. He focused his mind on his firing skill, he knew he was a crack shot, he wasn't going to let that man die. He steeled his nerves against the doubt and aimed at Leo's exposed shoulder. He fired.

Leo screamed and spun around to the ground. The guard, now free from Leo's threat, turned and grabbed his gun from Leo as Doyle and the first guard came running up. Doyle said, "Cuff him, I have to check my partner to see if he's all right. I'll explain what this is all about shortly."

Having heard gunfire, other officers, both State Police and capital building cops came running from elsewhere in the building. Doyle was on his way back to where he left Sara and Oscar. He found them both sitting on the bench, Sara looked disturbed. She stood and asked, "What happened to my father?"

Doyle walked up and told her to sit and started questioning her. "Sara, explain to me where you got the lottery ticket."

"My father bought it at the grocery store. I was with him when he bought it. I didn't know it was a winner until he came back and told me I had to turn it in. He was an ex-con and he didn't think they'd allow him to accept the money. I agreed to turn it in, and we'd split the winnings. I didn't know about the other winners, until Mr. Drew told me just now. Do you think my father actually murdered those people?"

"We do. I'm sorry, but the evidence points to him," Doyle replied.

"Who was the man in the basement?"

"I think he was going to buy the lottery ticket from your father so your father wouldn't have to turn it in. I think your father got greedy and took the money offered by Wasserman, then killed him. He decided to confide in you about the winnings and had you turn them in."

"Where is my father now?" she asked, almost in tears. Doyle felt for the woman, thanks to her father, she'd been through the ringer.

"He's being held by the police for now. He'll have some explaining to do, and have to answer for what he did." Doyle thought about the ticket and told her, "Look, despite what your father did, you should go collect for the winnings. You may need it to hire a lawyer."

Doyle's Law

A woman came out of the lottery office and announced that they would start the ceremony. Doyle stood and helped Sara up. "Oscar, escort Sara into the room and stay with her."

Oscar said he would and took her to the door. Doyle stood, watching them go in. He turned back to go talk to the police about Leo. He wasn't looking forward to that.

An hour later, Sara had her check for the money she agreed on. Not all of it, since Uncle Sam had to get his cut, and she took a lump sum instead of the timed payments. She took home a lot less than the announced winnings, but everybody else had to get their cut of the money, too. But, she walked away set for life. Doyle had to endure interrogation by investigators and told them to call Detective Howard Jones at the Sterling Heights PD for verification of his story.

Doyle finally finished with the police and went back to the lottery office. He found Oscar and Sara back on the bench. She stood when he came up.

"What about my father?" she asked.

He really hated to tell her that she would be without him again, but Leo made his choices. Some criminals just don't learn.

"He's in police custody until they can sort this all out. It will take a while, but I'm afraid your father may go back to prison. I'm sorry."

She looked crushed, but stood tall and smiled. "Well, he wasn't the best father a girl could want. I'm sorry for him, but he was wrong and should be punished."

"Good attitude to have. Keep thinking that way and you'll be fine. Now, how'd you get here?"

"I drove with my father in our car," she replied.

"Excuse me for a moment," he said and told Oscar to follow him. They went aside and Doyle said, "Why don't you drive Sara back home. I don't think she's ready to drive alone all that way."

"Sounds good, Art, I'll take care of her. You going to take care of Leo?"

"Yeah, they have to decide what to do about him. He'll be wanted in three cities for murder and for attacking a capital building officer. Everyone is going to want a piece of him. I'll stay until they figure out who has jurisdiction."

"Okay, I'll see you back in Detroit." Oscar turned and told Sara he was taking her home. She smiled and the two of them went back down the hallway to the entrance.

Doyle watched them go and went back to the capital police office. Doyle was told by a State Police lieutenant that they would escort Leo back down to Sterling Heights, where Wasserman was killed. Since they had a body connected to Leo, they would take charge of the man.

Doyle was glad it was all over, he went to his Charger and drove out. He was tooling down the freeway listening to a classic radio station blaring out Steppenwolf's '*Born to Be Wild*' and singing along.

About an hour later, and after a stop at Burger King, he got to the office. It was almost four o'clock and he found Marge was still there.

171

"I didn't expect you to be back so soon. Did everything work out?" Marge asked after Doyle came in through the back door.

"Well, Leo won't be happy, and Sara is going to lose her father again, but everything turned out fine," Doyle said as he sat in his desk chair. "Everything quiet here?"

"Oh yes. You need to advertise more. Get more clients in," Marge said with a grin.

"I'll look into it. Look up the advertising department of the Free Press and the News so I can call them tomorrow."

She said she would and pulled out the phone book. While she was looking, the phone rang and she answered. "Doyle Private Investigations. May I help you?" She listened then put the caller on hold. "You have a Detective Jones from Sterling Heights calling for Oscar."

"I'll take it, Marge, thanks." He hit the button to answer. "Howard, Art Doyle here. Oscar isn't in right now, what can I do for you?"

"The state police dropped off Kellogg. I got him into interrogation and the man is really a prize. He told me a tale about his daughter being the ring leader in the murders."

That sent a chill through his body. "Talk to me," Doyle said.

*

Chapter 26

"The state police dropped off Leo and I had him taken to interrogation. The man was a ball of nerves. He fidgeted the whole time he was in there. I finally talked to him about Wasserman. Oh, I had a nice talk with the Detroit police about them finding Wasserman. Seems they canvased the area where he was found and talked to an old man who lived next door to Leo. He said he saw two men carrying Wasserman out the back door of Leo's house and watched them deposit him two houses down. He waited until they left and called the police. I wonder who those two men could be?"

"Hmm, haven't a clue," Doyle replied, grinning.

"Well, back to Leo, I was grilling him about the four dead people and telling him his options for conviction. The death penalty in Michigan was deemed unconstitutional in 1964, so I told him he would probably get life without parole. He really started to fidget worse then. He blurted out that it was his daughter who set up the killings of the lottery winners and had some boyfriend do the killing."

"Boyfriend? Did Leo say who?"

"Yeah, Leo's bookie, some guy named Louis."

Doyle's Law

Doyle about fell out of his chair. Son-of-a-bitch, he thought, damn that Louis. "Okay, what else?"

"Before all the murders, Leo found Wasserman through some unsavory friends who dealt with money laundering and stolen goods. They told Leo that Wasserman might help him. He approached Wasserman and made a deal to sell him the ticket in exchange for quick cash. Leo admits killing Wasserman, but firmly denied the other murders. He says his daughter got greedy and wanted all the money and not share it. So she brought in Louis to take care of the other winners."

"How did she find out about the others?"

"Called the lottery people, claiming she was a reporter and wanted the names of the winners. They really shouldn't give out the names before awarding the money."

"So, Leo said Sara is the one who set up the murders. Devious bitch," Doyle said, thinking about Oscar being with Sara. "Thanks for that, I have to call Oscar, he's with Sara. I hope he's alright."

"If I get anything more from him, I'll call. Find Oscar, and we'll talk later." He hung up and Doyle pulled out his cell phone. He hit speed dial for Oscar and waited as it rang on the other end. It rang far too long. Oscar always answered his phone after two rings. He had no idea where to start looking for them. He thought about going to Sara's house, so he stood and told Marge he was going out.

"If Oscar comes in, tell him to call me immediately." He went out the back door to his car and drove out. He arrived at the house and but didn't know what kind of car Sara had. There were two parked out front of the house. He hoped Oscar was there.

He saw Jesse James on his front lawn watering the sparse grass that was mostly brown. He got out of his car and went to Jesse.

"Hey Doyle, did you find Sara and her father?" Jesse asked.

"You haven't seen either of them today?" he asked back.

"Nope, but I haven't been watching since I've been out shopping for food."

"Who do these cars belong to?" Doyle asked.

"Don't know, never saw them before."

"Anyone in the house that you noticed?"

"Nope, it's been quiet around there." Jesse turned off the water and said, "Damn grass just won't grow."

"Maybe because it's September and getting cold. Thanks Jesse, I'll check the house." Doyle said and went to the house. He knocked on the door, holding on to his Sig under his jacket. He knocked again but no one answered.

Doyle went around back and up to the back door. He carefully pushed it open, it still was not secure. He called in, "Anyone here?" and got no answer. He drew his gun and carefully walked into the kitchen. He peeked around into the dining room and saw no one. He checked the rest of the house and it was empty.

He went back out and waved to Jesse as the man was still watering his grass. He got into the car and sat thinking. Maybe they would go to her credit union to cash the check. But that amount of money would take time for the bank to process. If they even had enough to give her. He wondered if Sara got Oscar in her clutches, or was she just waiting until she had the money before she did anything to him.

He tried calling Oscar again and got nothing. Now he was worrying about his friend.

He called the office and Marge answered. "Marge, look up on the computer any credit unions within five miles of my location." He gave her the address and waited. She came back on and said there was one. She gave him the location and he thanked her.

The credit union wasn't far, which was good. He drove away from Sara's house and over to the credit union. He pulled into the parking lot and, again, didn't know what car to look for. He got out and went into the building, finding an area with desks and people who looked like bank officers. He went to the closest.

"Excuse me, but can you help me?" Doyle asked a woman at a desk. She stood and walked around the desk to him.

"What is it you need?" she asked.

Doyle took out his investigators ID and showed her. "I had an associate of mine bring in a young woman to cash her lottery winnings. He was protecting her. Do you know if they came in?"

"Do you mean Sara Kellogg?"

"Yes, that's her. Was she already here?"

"Oh, yes. We couldn't help her with such an amount to cash. She had to deposit the check and we told her to come back tomorrow so we could arrange for that amount of cash to be brought in from our main office. She wasn't happy, but had to agree."

"Great, was my associate with her?"

"If you mean the man with the funny attitude, he had our staff in stiches. Yes, he was with her."

Doyle was glad that Oscar was alright so far. "How long ago did they leave?"

"About a half hour ago. The man said something about getting some food."

That sounded like Oscar. "Thank you so much for your help." He handed her his card and said, "If they come back, please call me immediately. It's important."

She said she would and Doyle left. He sat in his car wondering where they would go to eat. So far, Sara hadn't let on that she was the culprit in this crime. He thought about Louis, figuring he may know something. Doyle started the car and drove to the pool hall. He arrived there and went in. There wasn't any tournament going on so there weren't as many people in the building.

He looked around for Louis but didn't see him. "Hey, aren't you that friend of Val's?" he heard someone say.

He turned to find a waitress behind him. "Yes, I'm Val's friend. How did you know?"

"I saw you here that first night you two met. Val told me she had a date with a big P.I. and was going to see you later that night. How is she? I haven't heard from her since she quit."

"She's doing very well. I saw her just this morning."

"I'll bet you did," she replied with a sly smile.

"Say, can you tell me where I might find Louis the bookie?"

"What do you want with that slimeball?" she asked.

"I have a few questions to ask him. He isn't around is he?"

"No, but he has a crib down the street. I can give you the address."

"That would be great," he said and took out his notebook. She wrote the address in the book and handed it back to him.

"If you and Val don't work out, I'm free."

Doyle smiled and said, "I have a partner you may like. He's a P.I. like me."

"Well, send him around and tell him to see Mandy."

"I will Mandy. Thanks for the info." He left her and went back to his car.

The building was run down and looked like it was built in the early 30s. He parked on the street and went to the door. It was a nail salon, probably a front for his bookie operations. He entered and a woman asked him, "What can we do for you? You need your nails polished?"

"No thank you, I'm looking for Louis," he said and watched her face. She smiled and pointed to a door in the back. He went to the door and tried it, but it was locked. He looked back as the woman pushed a button at her station. The door buzzed and Doyle opened it.

He had his Sig in hand as he entered the room. There were a couple rows of desks with phones on them. There were about four men in the room at the desks, probably taking bets. He looked around and saw a small office off the side with a large window looking out to the main room. He saw Louis sitting, facing away, so he didn't see Doyle come in.

Doyle went to the room and through the door. Louis turned just in time to see Doyle pounce on him, grabbing his bolo tie and pulling him out of his chair. Louis was gurgling as Doyle pulled him out of the room and over an empty desk.

"Now Louie, let's talk about Sara," he growled, pushing Louis' face into the desktop.

*

Chapter 27

Doyle turned Louis over on the desk to his back. Doyle looked to the four men in the room and aimed his Sig at them. "Get out now!" he yelled to them. They all looked surprised and stood, leaving Doyle and Louis alone. Doyle put the gun to Louis' head and pressed. "Talk to me about Sara!" he yelled into Louis' face.

"Geez, Doyle, I left her alone like you said. What more do you want?" he squirmed and tried to talk, his voice raspy from Doyle pulling tightly on his bolo tie. "Come on, Doyle, I can't breathe."

"I'll squeeze the air out of you, you scumbag. I know all about the murders of the lottery winners, we have Leo in custody for Wasserman's murder. Now, you want to tell me about the other three people who died because of you and Sara?"

Leo's eyes were bugging out, so Doyle eased up a bit more. "Hey, it was the bitch's idea to eliminate the competition, not me. I just provided the muscle to take care of them. I didn't do anything, blame my men. It was them that did the deeds, not me."

"Maybe you didn't commit the murders, but you are going down for accessory to murder. I want to see you dance in jail while the other inmates make you do a cake walk. They'll just love your tiny ass, Louie."

"What do you want, Doyle?" Louis whined. "My confession? My confession is that Sara is a ruthless bitch. That she orchestrated this whole deal and got the book on poison from her father. She gave me the poison to use, and told us to use different methods to kill the winners, so it looked random, she said. I'll freely give my statement to the police, just remember that."

"If Sara isn't at her house, where would I find her?" Doyle asked, pulling the tie again.

"I don't know, Doyle! Stop choking me!" He was turning purple now.

Doyle let up and asked again, "Where would I find her?"

"If she's not home, try her brother's house."

"Brother? Why didn't she mention him?" Doyle was surprised and he didn't like it.

"They don't talk much anymore. They had a falling out, but she occasionally goes to see him. She told him she had some money for him and he got real friendly."

"Where's he at?"

"If you stop choking me and let me up, I'll give you the info."

Doyle pulled the man up by his tie and led him to another desk. He picked up a pen and paper and handed them to Louis. "Hey, I don't know his address right off, I have to get my contact list."

"Where is it?"

"In my office."

Doyle pulled him there and said to start writing. Louis pulled a book out of his desk and opened it. He thumbed through pages and stopped. He read the entry and then wrote the address on the sheet of paper.

Doyle looked out the window of the office into the other room and saw the locked door open, in came two huge men with guns. Doyle dove down, moved over to the ledge of the window, and shot through it. The glass shattered, raining down on the floor. Doyle noticed he caught one of the men in the side. They brought up their guns and started firing at the office. Doyle dropped to the floor hoping the bullets didn't penetrate the wood walls where he was at.

Louis was screaming, "You idiots! I'm in here, stop firing!"

They couldn't hear Louis hiding on the ground behind the desk, while they were busy blasting the room. Doyle belly-crawled to the door and fired around the corner at the only man in view. Doyle's shot hit him in the leg, the man screamed and went down. He peeked his head around the door and spotted the other shooter. Blood was staining the man's shirt and he was having difficulty shooting due to the gunshot wound in his side. Bullets were flying, but way off mark. Doyle suspected the man wasn't going to hold out for long, so he held his fire. The shooter proved Doyle correct when he grabbed his side and toppled over onto the floor.

Doyle stayed still until he was sure they were out for the count. He rolled over and found himself staring into a short-barrel shotgun held by Louis. He stood right over Doyle.

"Now who has the advantage, wise guy?" Louis said with glee.

Doyle smiled and brought his leg up into Louis' balls. He screamed and fell away from Doyle, who pushed up and grabbed the shotgun away from Louis.

"You are a pathetic little man, Louie. They'll love you in prison." Doyle went to him and pulled his arms around his back and strapped his wrists with a zip cuff. Then he did the same to his legs. Doyle pulled his cell phone and called a friend on the force that he knew.

Twenty minutes later three uniforms and Doyle's detective friend, Josh Morris, arrived. "I can't hang around, I have to find Oscar. He may be in trouble," Doyle explained quickly.

"Go, can't let Oscar get hurt. Do you need back up?" Morris asked.

"I'll be alright," Doyle said.

Morris looked at the men on the floor being treated by the EMTs and said, "I can see that. You know you'll have to answer for this mess."

"Later, I really got to go." They finished up and Doyle went out to his car. He looked at the address Louis had written down and raced away.

Doyle drove out to the city of Harper Woods - near his apartment - where he found the street. He drove slowly, trying to find the address. He spotted it and parked out front. There were no other cars on the street, which worried him.

He went around the side of the house trying to see in the windows, hoping a neighbor didn't poke a shotgun in his face. He could hear noises inside the house, people talking loudly, but couldn't see anyone. He went to the back door and tried the knob. It wasn't locked.

He cautiously pushed the door open and stood listening. He heard men's voices, but no women. The chatter was coming from another room, so he pulled his Sig and entered the kitchen. He moved carefully to the door opening and peeked around the corner. He saw two men sitting in what looked like a living room, but it had mattresses on the floor and was a mess with trash everywhere.

He didn't see Sara or Oscar, and thought maybe they didn't come here. He was watching the men when he felt a presence behind him. He spun around with his gun out and found a young girl wearing only a t-shirt. She jumped when she saw the gun and screamed.

He heard movement in the other room, so he pulled the girl over to the opening to the living room and stood back waiting for the attack. They came up behind the girl and looked surprised.

"What the hell, is this a robbery?" one man said.

Doyle brought his Sig up and yelled, "Shut up, I'm not here to rob you, I want to know where Sara Kellogg is."

"You going to kill my sister, man?" the other guy said.

Doyle said, "Is she here?"

"No, man, she was, but left."

"How long ago and was there a man with her?"

"Yeah, he was hanging around to take her wherever she wanted to go. He was a real comic, he a friend of yours?"

Doyle looked into their eyes and could see they were high. He started to smell grass burning and figured they were harmless stoners. "Do you know where they went?"

"I heard Sara say she wanted to go shopping. Maybe they went to the mall."

Doyle was wondering what Sara was up to, and if Oscar knew what he was up against yet. He would never let her get the jump on him, he hoped. "Is she staying here or going back to her home?"

"She didn't say. She gave me some money and said she may be back. We got some good weed with the money, you aren't a cop are you? You look like a cop."

"I'm not a cop, but don't get caught." Doyle turned and went out the back door to his car.

He was sitting, thinking about what to do next when his cell phone rang. He looked at the caller ID and saw it was Oscar. He felt relieved and answered. "Oscar, where are you?"

There was silence, than he heard a woman's voice, saying "Shut up and listen." It was Sara.

*

Chapter 28

"If you harm Oscar, I will hunt you down," Doyle growled into the phone.

"Yeah, yeah, tough guy. I like Mr. Drew, I wouldn't harm him. As long as you cooperate," she replied.

"Cooperate? Doing what?" he asked.

"Well, I'm sure by now my dear old loving daddy has spilled his guts about this whole mess and the murders. Turns out killing the other winners didn't help. The relatives of the dead all wanted their share of the winnings. Since none of the people killed left a will about the winnings, the lottery people have to sort it out to see where the money goes. To the heirs of the victims or the state, but I didn't get it. Although I still have enough money to live on comfortably for a very long time. But, I still have to get the money from the credit union without being stopped by the cops. That's where you come in."

"So you expect me to cooperate?" he asked.

"You will if you want Mr. Drew back. I have him secured at a location only known to me. He's safe for now, but if I'm stopped from getting my money and making a clean getaway, I'll let him die a slow death by starvation. We both know he loves to eat and I won't tell you where he is at." She paused to let it sink into Doyle. "Now, here's how I want this to go. So far, according to Mr. Drew, I understand that you know where I bank. Did you tell the police?"

"No," he said.

"Good, now in the morning I'm going to the credit union to get my money. I don't want to see any police, or you, around when I go. Your friend will remain here, tied up and waiting to be rescued. When I have my money and I drive safely away, I'll call you with the location of your friend. Simple as that."

"How do I know you'll call?" Doyle pressed.

"I happen to like Mr. Drew. He's a nice man and really funny too, so I don't really want to see him harmed. Unless, you don't do what I say, then it won't be pleasant."

186

"Agreed, but you better call," Doyle said quietly.

"Or what? You'll hunt me down? I'll have enough money to disappear easily enough. To places you couldn't afford to go, so don't threaten. Just do what I say and everything will be fine." She hung up.

"Bitch," Doyle spat out. He sat back thinking about his next move and realized he had none. He knew he would be at the credit union early in the morning, watching for her to collect the money. But, where was she keeping Oscar? She still had the money they took from Wasserman. With that she could have taken him anywhere.

Doyle's cell phone rang out *Jaws* and the caller ID said private. He answered hoping it was Oscar on another phone. "Hello," he said.

"Mr. Doyle? This is Jesse James. You said to call if I saw Sara or her father. Well, Sara got back here a few minutes ago. She's still here and in her house."

"Thanks Jesse, I'm on my way. Don't talk to her, it turns out she's dangerous and has a gun. She's wanted for three murders, so stay away."

Jesse sounded surprised, "I haven't talked to her yet, but I won't."

"Was she alone or with someone?" Doyle asked.

"She was with that no good brother of hers. The drugged out one. He's really a waste of life. There was no one else with them, just the two. Want I should stop them with my shotgun?"

"Oh, hell, no. She's hiding my partner somewhere and I need her alive to tell me where he's at. Just watch them from your window and keep an eye on what they're doing. I'll be right over." He hung up and speed dialed Josh Morris with the info. "Josh, I got a location on Sara Kellogg. She's back at her house." Doyle gave him the address and said he was heading there. He hung up hoping someone would get to her.

On the way, he thought this might be a bad move. If Oscar was hidden somewhere, and they grabbed Sara now, she wouldn't tell where she had him. That could be a bad thing to do. He dialed back his friend and explained the situation.

"I'm going to go there, but I'll stay back and see where they go and follow them. They may go back to Oscar."

"I'll call the cars to back off, let me know what happens," Josh said and hung up.

Doyle came to the street, but didn't drive down it. He stopped at the curb of the cross street and watched down at the house. There was a car in front, but he had no idea if it was hers. He pulled his cell phone and hit redial for Jesse.

"Jesse James here, what do you want?" he answered. Evidently Jesse didn't have caller ID.

"Jesse, it's Doyle. Are they still in the house?

"Yep. They haven't come out yet. I'm still watching. Are you coming?"

"No, it may be harmful for my friend if I show up. So, I'm down the street watching. I'll follow them to see where they go. Keep watching and tell me if they leave. I don't think they will stay long, since I know where she lives, she may figure I'll end up there. Stay on the line until you see something."

"I'll yell if I see movement," Jesse said.

Doyle put the phone on speaker and waited. About ten minutes later, Jesse yelled through the phone, "They're coming from around the back, walking towards the car. They've got luggage, she must be getting ready to run."

"Okay, Jesse, thanks, I'll take it from here." He hung up as he saw the two of them going to the car. He pulled his binoculars from under his seat and made a note of the license plate number. He wrote it down and continued to watch. They loaded the trunk with the luggage and then got in the car. He watched them drive away.

He pulled away from the curb and followed carefully. His cherry red Charger wasn't difficult to spot, so he held way back. It wasn't the first time he tailed someone, but he was usually in an unmarked police car. They moved down to the main road and turned right. Doyle sped up to get to the corner, he saw them and he pulled out into traffic. Luckily traffic was heavy, but not so much that he couldn't still see them.

Suddenly, he heard sirens and looked in his rear view mirror, it was a fire engine, a big one. He had to pull over to let it go by. He was trying to keep an eye on Sara's vehicle, but the bright red truck blocked his view. By the time it was down the road and out of the way, Sara was gone.

"Damn!" he yelled and hit the steering wheel. He drove on, looking around to see if he could spot them. He pulled into an Arby's and parked. He dialed Josh again.

"Josh, I lost them, but I got the plate number and make of the car. If you could put out a BOLO to just observe where they are, but not stop them, it would be a big help."

"I'll take care of it, give me the info," Doyle repeated the plate number and make of the car to him.

"Give me a call if they're spotted and let me know their twenty. I lost them on Clairmount by Rosa Parks Boulevard, heading east."

"That'll help. I'll call you as soon as I get a fix on them. Be careful." They finished and hung up.

Doyle sat feeling helpless and he didn't like it. He always liked to feel in control, even in high-pressure situations. Ever since the mayor's shooting, he felt a little less in control. He didn't like the fact that hitting the mayor had shaken him up so much. He always felt that hitting an innocent victim of a crime was wrong. He would never shoot a victim.

He looked around and decided to drive back to the office. Since the police were on watch for the car, he could take a quick breather for a bit. He drove out of the Arby's, went back to the office and parked in back.

He entered through the back door, noticing the lock Oscar installed started him thinking about his friend. He hoped he was alright. If Sara did anything to him, she would pay. Marge was at her desk and smiled when Doyle came up.

"So, where's Oscar?" she asked.

Doyle realized that she wasn't aware of what was happening. He pulled over a chair and sat.

"I have some news to tell you. Nothing bad so far, but I have to take care of it." He told her everything from their time in Lansing to now. She sat nodding her head and started to look upset.

"Oh, dear. That's not good. Do you think the police will spot her car?"

"I hope so, I can't believe I lost her. At least I know she'll be at the credit union in the morning, so that'll give me another chance to get to Oscar. I'll be there and I won't let her get away this time." He stood and went to a stack of boxes in the back filled with things they hadn't unpacked for the business. He dug around and found what he was looking for. He smiled and went to his desk. He played with the electronic device and got it working. He would need it tomorrow.

*

Chapter 29

Doyle told Marge to go home, he'd lock up.

"I'd hate to leave not knowing if Oscar is going to be safe. I'll wait for a little bit longer," she said.

"I don't think anything will develop until tomorrow morning. Either Sara will call after she gets her money or I'll have to stop her and torture her," he said with a grin, trying to break the tension.

Marge laughed slightly and said, "You're right. I guess my being here isn't going to speed up the process." She gathered her things and stood. "I'll be in early tomorrow morning. Her credit union doesn't open until nine."

"And I'll be there at eight-forty, waiting. I'll see you in the morning," Doyle said. Marge left, going out the back door. He got up and went to lock the front and back doors.

He sat back at his desk and called Josh Morris on his cell phone. He waited until his friend answered.

"Art, we haven't gotten anything on the car yet, sorry," Josh said, when he answered.

"I'm trying to make a plan here. I got a tracking device that I've had for years. It still works and I'm going to put it on her car in the morning when she goes to collect her money. I'm not going to lose her again."

"Is that your entire plan?"

"No, I'll need your help. I'm trying to think of places she would put Oscar and I was wondering if you can get a warrant to search her brother's house tomorrow after she goes to the credit union?"

"I can arrange it. Anywhere else?"

"Might be a good idea to check her home, too. May as well cover all bases. I'll give you the addresses and if you can wait until I call to let you know what is happening tomorrow, I'd appreciate it."

"I'll get the warrants and wait. I hope Oscar is all right."

192

"So do I. I'd hate to have to break in a new partner," Doyle said.

"I'll get the ball rolling. If you need anything else, call."

Doyle gave Josh the addresses and they finished.

He sat back trying to organize his plan. He laughed to himself thinking this would be plan B, just for Oscar. There was nothing more he could do, Sara had the upper hand for now. He gathered his things and went out the back door.

He drove back to his apartment and found Val waiting for him by her car. "I'll have to get you a key so you don't have to keep sitting out here in the parking lot," he said as he kissed her.

After they were in his apartment, she handed him a small gift-wrapped package. He smiled and said, "Is it my birthday?"

"Just open it," she grinned.

He went to the couch to sit and unwrap the gift. He opened the box and found a shiny badge saying "Private Investigator."

"I got it from one of Ken's old police catalogs for cop accessories. They even included P.I. stuff. I had it shipped over night."

"Well, this is special. Thank you. Can you order another for Oscar?" he asked.

She smiled and opened her purse, pulling out another box, not gift wrapped. "I already thought of it."

"You keep this up and I may think about marrying you."

"Think about?"

"I'm not sold on marriage anymore. I've been there once and it was good, but I don't know if I can go through it again. Let's just play house until we really get to know each other. You may hate me in six months and divorces are really messy nowadays."

She laughed and kissed him. "Have you found Oscar yet?" she asked on a more somber note.

He set the badges aside and said, "No, and I'm really worried. I hope Sara doesn't screw up her deal. I don't know where to look for him. I've called a friend of mine in for reinforcements though. He'll do a couple raids in the morning to see if he can find Oscar."

"Where?"

"At Sara's house and her brother's," he replied.

"Do you think she would hide Oscar in obvious places?"

"No, I don't, but it's possible she's not that clever. She knows we won't go busting in before she gets her money and calls me… or not, so it's possible she won't care if we do find him."

"How's she going to get away? If you find Oscar, can't you stop her?"

"I don't know how she plans to get away. She'll have tons of money; she could charter a jet to get away. I'm putting a tracker on her car, so we'll be able to follow her wherever she goes. This all has to go in a timed plan, or she could clam up and we'd never find Oscar."

"I have faith that you'll find him."

"Thanks, I need to try and get to sleep, to make the day go faster. I'm sure I won't, I'll be worrying all night."

"Let's go snuggle, it may help you sleep."

He smiled and stood, pulling her up. "It's early, but I need the rest." They went to the bedroom.

Doyle slept, but was having bad dreams. Sara had Doyle tied up and was flailing him with a bull whip. He felt the sting every time she struck out, but he wouldn't cry out. Finally, he looked around and she was gone, but he found himself in a burned out building, smoke still rising up from the charred wood. He looked down and found he was on fire. Now he cried out.

Val was shaking him as he sat up in bed. "Art, wake up."

He looked to her, breathing heavily. "I guess I may not want to go back to sleep," he said looking at the clock by his bed. It was only six-fifty. "I need to get ready to go," he said, getting out of the bed and going to the bathroom.

A short time and a shower later, he was dressed and getting ready to go. Val made breakfast for herself, she knew he didn't eat breakfast, so more for her. He came out from the bedroom and gave her a kiss.

"Thanks for being with me this morning, it helps."

"Go and find Oscar. You need this."

"I will, or Sara is going to regret ever hiring us." He kissed her again and left. He started his car and drove to the office.

Doyle's Law

Marge was already in and waiting. Doyle didn't feel like going through the mail so he got the tracking device ready. It had a large earth magnet attached to it, so he could just slap it on the car and it would stay on even through rough driving.

He called Josh to see if he got the warrants. "Got them this morning. We're ready to go. Do you think Oscar could be in either place?" Josh asked.

"I haven't the faintest idea, but they're places to look. I don't think Sara would go to a lot of trouble to hide him. Even if she doesn't call, she probably figures we'll go to the houses and find him. She said she didn't want to hurt Oscar, he does have a tendency to grow on people. I don't care if she gets away with the money, as long as she returns Oscar."

"Well, the money is hers. But she'll have a hard time spending it from prison. Call me when it's time to pull the raids. I have two teams waiting."

"Thanks, Josh, I appreciate your help."

"Like you said, Oscar grows on you. I like the guy and don't want to see him hurt. Talk later," he said and hung up.

Doyle looked at his watch, it was now eight-thirty and he figured he'd get a start on it. He told Marge that he was leaving, she wished him luck. He went out to his car and drove to the credit union. He parked in the next lot of a restaurant and waited. He would see what car they came in and would go attach the tracker to it. He knew they would be inside the credit union for a while to get that amount of money.

Bob Moats

He checked the laptop he brought to keep track of where they went. The tracker was showing his location, so it was working. He sat back and waited.

About twenty minutes later, after the employees had shown up, he saw a car slowly approaching and pulling in. He could see two people, a man and a woman, it had to be them. They parked and got out. He saw that it was indeed Sara and her brother as they walked across the parking lot to the glass doors. Keep it in the family, Sara, you bitch, he thought.

They went into the building, so Doyle got out and went along the front of the cars in the lot to the one they came in. He leaned down and put the tracker under the front of the car. It grabbed onto the metal body and stuck. He stood and went back to his car.

The program on the laptop showed the new location of the tracker, he was happy. He called Josh and gave him and update.

"Can you give me the frequency of the tracker, we can use the equipment in our cars to follow," Josh asked.

"Good idea," Doyle said and gave them the frequency. Josh said they had a fix on it. "I'll call after they finish and see if she calls or not. Be ready to move." They finished the call and Doyle sat back waiting for them to come out.

*

Chapter 30

Doyle sat for a good forty-five minutes, when he saw the two of them coming out of the building. The brother was carrying a large gym bag that he had taken in. Now it looked full. They got in their car and drove out.

Doyle didn't have to rush, he had them on the screen of his laptop heading east. He was wondering where they were heading to. He called Josh and said they were on the move.

"I got them on screen. Where do you think they would go?" Josh asked.

Doyle was thinking about ways they could go on the run. He was watching the screen and trying to drive. He had to be careful not to get in an accident. He saw they were on Caniff still heading east. He pulled over and took out his Detroit map and looked around that area, then he saw it.

He picked up his phone and said, "Josh, I think they are heading for the old Detroit City Airport. It's the only thing I can see in the direction they're going."

"Do you want me to get some cars out there?"

"No, but be ready to call them. I'm going to call Sara on Oscar's cell phone. She had it last, so I hope she still does. I'll keep you up on things." He hung up and speed dialed Oscar's cell. It rang for a long time until the voice mail kicked in. He hung up. "Damn her. She's not going to call." Then he thought she might call when she was on her way out of town. If she was taking a plane.

He started his car again and drove in the direction of the airport. He finally came within sight of it and saw that the tracker placed them at the airport also. He drove to the entrance and in. He didn't know which private flight she was taking, there were a number of carriers. He adjusted his screen to zoom in on the tracker. He saw it was right in front of him. He drove carefully towards a hanger with an office next to it. A sign on the building said, "Karlin Charter Flights" and then he saw Sara and her brother going into the building.

He pulled around the side and got out. He watched as a small Cessna plane was being pulled out of the hanger. He waited to see what was going to happen next. About ten minutes later, Sara and her brother came out of the office with another man. They stood talking and then went towards the plane.

Doyle felt conflicted. Should he stop them or let them go, figuring that Sara would call once they were away? She had to have seen that he was trying to call Oscar's phone earlier. Did she just ignore it or did she not have the phone? Which meant she didn't plan to call, he wasn't even sure if she had her own phone. They were standing by the plane as the pilot was doing his pre-flight check.

Doyle pulled out his cell phone and speed dialed Oscar's phone again. He watched Sara and heard no phone ringing. Sara didn't move to look at a phone, so that told Doyle she didn't have it. "Hell with it, I'll take my chances," he said out loud to himself, then he called Josh and said to send in the troops, and ran to the plane. Sara and her brother had their backs to him and he had his Sig out as he came up.

"Sara!" he yelled. She jumped and turned towards him. Her eyes grew wide when she realized it was him.

"You were told not to come near us, you've just killed your partner," she spat out.

"Really?" Doyle said and came closer. He shot at her brother's leg and he screamed, dropping the bag and falling to the ground. "Maybe I'll kill your brother. How about that?"

The pilot saw this and ran back to the hanger.

She stood stone-faced and said, "Go ahead, I was going to get rid of him anyway. He was useless baggage to me. I don't need him or anyone. I'm rich now and I can do anything I want."

"What makes you think you can get away now?"

"First, I know where Mr. Drew is, and secondly, you should drop your gun."

"And why should I do that?" Doyle asked.

"Because I'll shoot you if you don't," came a voice from behind him. He looked back and saw the pilot with a rifle. "I usually use this to shoot birds on the runway, but I can shoot you just as easily."

"Do you know why you're doing this? This woman is wanted by the police for murdering three people. Are you part of her gang?"

He saw a flicker of confusion in the man's eyes. "What do you mean?" he asked.

"Just what I said, she's a wanted felon. Do you want to go down with her?"

The man started to slowly lower his rifle and was suddenly shot. Doyle spun back and saw Sara had a gun. Oscar's favorite .38 and was now aiming at Doyle. He still had his Sig aimed at her and said, "Well, we have a standoff." He could hear the man behind him was still alive.

In the distance they could hear the sirens of the approaching police. "Well, the cavalry is coming and you shot your pilot. Now what are you going to do. Fly the plane yourself?"

"No, I'm going to kill you." She brought the gun up to a firing position, Doyle had no other choice but to fire. He managed to hit her in the shoulder of her gun arm. She screamed and dropped to her knees, holding her shoulder. Doyle rushed to her and picked up Oscar's gun. The police cars came speeding up, parked and he saw Josh get out of one car. The two officers got out and stood around waiting for instructions.

"You missed the party, Josh," Doyle said.

He stood looking at the three people on the ground and said, "Why did you even bother calling us? You like to leave bodies on the ground. Talk to me."

"You better get a couple EMS units out here," Doyle said. "The guy behind me is a pilot, he thought he was saving her from me. She shot him."

"He's bleeding from his arm, so it looks like he'll live. Who's the kid?"

"Sara's brother. He was helping her get away. I shot him."

"And you shot her?"

"I had to, she was ready to shoot me." He took Oscar's gun out of his pocket. "This is Oscar's, she had it."

"But where's Oscar?"

Doyle looked to Sara. "Can I have a moment alone with her?"

"Sure, are you going to torture her?" Josh said with a grin.

"Not if she cooperates." He went to her and grabbed her good arm and pulled her up, she screamed and then Doyle dragged her to the hanger.

Once inside, he turned to her and said, "Oscar never did anything to you but be nice, and you treat him this way? You can't get away now, they'll have you for murder and kidnapping. That's a life sentence right there. Talk to me and I'll see what can be done for you."

"What? Get a couple years off my life sentence? How generous."

"Look, you didn't murder anyone directly, Louis set that up. He's going down for conspiracy to commit murder. Your father murdered Wasserman, so you're off that charge. The worse you could get is for organizing this whole mess. Give Oscar a break and tell me where he is."

She stared at him and said, "Screw you."

Doyle brought his fist back and slammed it into her face. She dropped and Doyle went out and to Josh. "She's all yours."

"Did she tell you where Oscar is?"

"No, send in your teams to the houses. See if he's there."

Josh got on his cell phone and placed the call after he told the offers to go get the woman. Doyle said he was going to her house to take a look, maybe find something that would help.

As Doyle was going to his car, Josh yelled, "You still have to answer for this mess."

"Later," Doyle yelled back and got in his car and drove off.

He arrived at Sara's house hoping to find anything that would give an answer to where she put Oscar. Jesse was watching from his front lawn and Doyle motioned to him to follow. The police were already checking the house over and didn't find Oscar.

"Damn, he has to be somewhere," Doyle said to Jesse. "You've been watching Sara, what has she been doing?"

"Well, her and that brother of hers were messing around the house the other day but nothing suspicious."

Doyle looked in the living room and saw a jacket on a chair. It looked like Oscar's. He picked it up and checked the pockets and found the list of winners in the lottery. It was Oscar's jacket. "Oscar would never have left his jacket just anywhere. He has to be here somewhere." He was noticing a smell. It was burnt wood. He smelled the jacket closely and said, "It's smoke. Where would he be that had smoke from burning wood?"

Doyle's Law

Suddenly both Jesse and Doyle smiled. Doyle called to the officers in the house. "Go search every burned out building on this side of the block, my partner has to be on one of them. Be sure to check the basements."

Everyone streamed out of the house and spread out. Jesse followed Doyle to the closest wreck and Doyle kicked in the back door. It gave way easily since the wood around it was well charred from the fire. Doyle went straight for the basement access and moved the burnt door away from the opening. He looked down and saw there was minimal damage to the stairs and went down calling Oscar's name.

He got to the bottom and looked to his right when he heard a muffled voice. He was filled with joy when he saw Oscar tied to a chair, tape over his mouth—but alive. Doyle rushed to him and pulled the tape.

Oscar took a breath and said, "What the hell took you so long?"

*

Chapter 31

"Don't be so snippy or I'll leave you tied up."

"No you won't, you love me too much," Oscar replied.

"We'll discuss that another time. Are you all right?"

"I've been tied to a chair in a stinky basement for God knows how long and you ask if I'm all right? I'm just peachy keen. Did you get Sara?"

"Yep, just as she was trying to take a private flight out of City Airport." He cut the ropes from Oscar's wrists.

"Did you shoot her? I hope you did."

"As a matter of fact, I did, but she's alive," Doyle said, taking Oscar's gun out of his pocket. "Here, you were probably missing this."

"Oh, baby, so good to see you." He kissed the gun and put it in the holster.

Doyle finished cutting the ropes holding Oscar's legs and asked, "Can you stand?"

Oscar tried to stand but wobbled and sat back down. "I need to stretch my legs, they're cramped up." He raised and lowered his legs as Doyle told Jesse to tell the police that he found Oscar. Jesse went back upstairs while Oscar tried to stand.

"Ow, that hurts," he said as he brought his body up straight. They went to the stairs and up, Doyle assisting Oscar.

"Good to see the sun again," Oscar said as they came out of the building. All the officers were gathering around expressing their feelings about Oscar being found.

Doyle took him to the car and stopped, calling Josh. He told him they found Oscar, then he called Marge to let her know Oscar was safe. She was very happy to hear that and said to say hi.

"So, you must have had a lot of time to think while you were down there," Doyle said as they drove away. "What revelations came up?"

"That I needed food. I'm still hungry, let's cruise the drive thru at the closest fast food place you see."

Doyle pulled into a McDonalds and they ordered.

Doyle bought extra burgers for Marge and they went back to the office. Marge went to Oscar and gave him a big hug. Doyle looked to his desk and was surprised to see Val siting in his chair. He went to her.

"How long have you been here?"

"Since about nine. I came to see if you found Oscar. I see you have." She stood and also gave Oscar a hug.

"Wow, maybe I'll get kidnapped more often," he joked.

Everyone was sitting as Oscar told them how Sara got the jump on him and they took him to the basement and tied him up. Doyle explained to Oscar what happened after he was hidden away.

"Shoulda shot her in the head," Oscar said, "She was one crazy bitch."

"Well, it's finished and everyone is tucked away in jail. Now we have to advertise and get this business moving."

Oscar stood and said, "I'm going home to crawl into my bed and sleep for a couple days."

"Do that, don't come back until you're rested."

Oscar went out the back door and Val said she was going to do some shopping. She kissed Doyle, said she'd see him later and left. Marge went back to her knitting as Doyle sat thinking about advertising.

The front door opened and in walked two large men and asked for Doyle. Marge looked to Doyle and he stood, "I'm Doyle," he said apprehensively.

They walked towards to him, but not too close. "We were asked by Louis to visit you. Seems he is not happy about the treatment you gave him or for putting him in jail. He asked us to take care of you." They took guns out of their pockets and held them out. "Louis sends his regards."

As the men stood there, they heard a clicking noise behind them and heard Marge say, "I wouldn't move if I were you. It would be detrimental to your health."

One man looked back and saw Marge pointing the huge .357 magnum at them. "Oh crap," the man said. The other man looked back and saw her.

Doyle moved quickly and took their guns, then clocked the closer man with his fist. The other man held his hands up and Doyle told him to turn around. He whacked the man in the head with the gun butt and he went down.

"Marge, call the police to clean up this mess. I guess you can bring your gun in anytime you want," he said with a grin.

"Next time I'll load it," she said. Doyle laughed out loud and said it would be a good idea.

Marge got on the phone, and ten minutes later the police arrived and took the men into custody. Doyle said he'd be in to press charges. He also wanted to visit Louis in his cell.

All was quiet again, Marge was at her desk cleaning and loading her gun as Doyle sat back looking around the room thinking about getting some nice walls.

THE END

*

Bob Moats

Join Doyle in his next adventure "Doyle's Justice". Here's a one chapter preview.

Chapter 1

Creeping quietly through the woods was made difficult due to the dead leaves of autumn covering the mossy ground. Every step resulted in a muted crackling sound that disturbed the silence of the late night three o'clock journey. The man dressed in black, to help hide his appearance, crept up behind the small log building to drop off the surprise for his old nemesis. His stealthy walk in the woods was being made more difficult by the body he was dragging. Even wrapped up in the plastic sheeting, the package was difficult to pull over the morning dew on the colorful rug of leaves.

The dark figure didn't care if it was hard to maneuver through the woods. He had a goal, a mission to deliver his gift. He finally broke through the stand of trees and into the small backyard of the building sitting empty in the moonlight. He knew the occupant was away, but his present would be there upon the resident's return. Removing the plastic sheeting, he set the body against the small wood pump house that provided well water for the cabin.

Doyle's Law

He turned the body to face the building and was delighted by the cleverness of his gift. A present to the one person he had a desire to involve in his murders, Arthur Doyle.

~~*~~

Doyle woke feeling a chill even though the temperature in his apartment was set at a steady seventy-eight degrees. He moved closer to the woman in bed with him for the body heat. She turned softly to meet his body and then put her arm over him, though she was still asleep. Instinct took over when one felt a closeness to another person. If she wasn't now used to the man in bed with her, she probably would have lashed out at Doyle. He knew to always be ready for an attack from his sleeping beauty.

Doyle lifted his head to look over the woman to see what time it was by the clock on the side bed stand. Three-thirty now and it was going to be hard to get back to sleep. Doyle was a light sleeper, a seemingly unbreakable habit from his former FBI training - be alert for any situation or attack by the enemy. He put his head back down and looked at Val, his sometimes live-in girlfriend, barely seeing her in the dim light of the outer room.

His mind went back to the day he met her in the pool hall while he was searching for a bookie. Not that he needed a bookie, but the creep was part of a missing person assignment Doyle had. Val was a waitress at the pool hall and they expressed a desire for each other. He had just broken up with another woman and he wondered if Val was only a rebound affair. She made him happy in many ways, mostly sexual, but she was intelligent and had a great sense of humor, too. She needed a sense of humor to be with Doyle.

He did fall back to sleep, totally unaware of what was happening fifty-two miles away at his cabin by Lake Metamora.

The next morning, he heard Val doing something in his kitchen. Probably making breakfast, which he didn't eat. He got up and dressed to go to the office of his private investigating business. Val had her own key to his apartment and would let herself out.

"Good morning," she said as he came out to her.

"Keep your good mornings to yourself," he grinned. "I didn't sleep very well and if it weren't for going out to solve crimes, I'd stay in bed," he said and kissed her lightly on the cheek.

She grabbed his shirt and pulled him back and planted a big kiss on his lips. "That's better," she said with a smile. He went to get his Sig Sauer 9 handgun and put it in the quick release holster under his left arm. He slid the new .38 in the holster behind him and looked in the mirror by the front door.

"I get older looking every day. I hate it," he said.

"You could stand to darken the grey in your hair. For a man of fifty-one, you're getting grey early."

"It makes me look wise and distinguished."

"It makes you look extinguished," she said with a subtle laugh.

"Whatever, I have to go to work. I'll talk to you later." He grabbed his jacket to cover his weapons and left the apartment. As he drove across the city of Detroit to his office, he thought about the affairs that brought him to his present state. He accidently shot the mayor of Detroit during a hostage exchange. Not a deadly shot, but it gave the mayor a nice scar on the side of his head so he'd always remember Doyle. He quit the Detroit police as a homicide detective after that. The job was getting to him and the incident with the mayor's outburst over being wounded was the final straw.

Doyle pulled up to the back of his building and went into the back door. He entered and found his partner, Oscar, talking to Marge, their secretary and receptionist.

"Hey Art, Marge and I were talking about ways to bring in more clients."

"More clients? If we get any more than we're getting now, I'll have to hire a couple ex-cops to help out. Since the advertising I've been doing, we've been doing nicely in the client department."

"True, but we need to keep up."

"What do you have going?" Doyle asked.

"Nothing glamorous, just following a cheating wife. Husband came in this morning and hired us."

"Well, it's a case. Surveillance is an art form," Doyle said.

"It is when you don't have to do it. I have to go follow the woman when she leaves for her yoga class this afternoon. I think she's probably bending her body for the instructor."

Marge laughed and said, "Since you opened for business last month, I'm getting to like this job. I've met some very interesting people."

"You evidently didn't get out much before," Doyle said.

"Actually, I didn't. I was too much of a housewife. While my late husband was out chasing criminals around Detroit, I was baking pies."

"Maybe someday you could bake us a nice apple pie," Oscar asked.

"You think too much about food, Oscar," Doyle said.

"Hey, I'm a growing boy," Oscar replied.

"Growing around the middle, yes. You need to keep in shape for any foot chases."

"Easier to shoot them than to run," Oscar said with grin.

"Do you realize all the interrogations and paperwork you have to go through when you fire your weapon and you're no longer a cop? I spent three days going over all that from the shootings I did over the Kellogg case. I'm using my wits and my fists from now on."

"Well, whatever, I have to go follow a wife. I hope she's good-looking, at least. Talk later." Oscar picked up a small briefcase and went out.

"How are you feeling this morning?" Marge asked.

"A little tired, didn't sleep well this morning. I felt a little uneasy and it was difficult to stay asleep."

"Something bothering you?"

"I don't know. It's just a feeling I have that something is wrong," Doyle said.

"Maybe you're developing a woman's intuition. I get those feelings, too, when something bad is going to happen."

"I won't mind the intuition, as long as I don't have other women's problems. I'm usually crabby, but not just once a month," he said, grinning.

"I'm too old now for that curse. At sixty-seven, arthritis is my curse."

The phone rang on Marge's desk, she answered. "Doyle Investigations, may I help you?" She listened and then said, "Please wait." She put the phone on hold and said to Doyle, "You have a call from a Sheriff Twain from out in Metamora. Isn't that where your cabin is?"

"Yes it is. Thanks, I'll take it at my desk." He went to his desk and was wondering why Mike Twain was calling him. He grew up with Mike in Oxford and they both went into law enforcement. Mike went to the county sheriff's department and

Doyle's Law

Doyle went to the FBI, then to Detroit police. He sat at his desk and hit the button on the phone.

"Mike, what's up?" he said.

"Art, got a problem. How soon do you think you can get up here?" the voice said in his ear.

"Well, it takes an hour to drive, why?"

"We got an anonymous call this morning that there was a body out back of your cabin. I'd like you to come and identify the body. We have no idea who she is."

Doyle knew that Gwen, his last girlfriend, was now in Cleveland, so it couldn't be her. "I can come right up, but give me some time to get organized."

"No problem. It's cold enough to keep the body presentable. We'll wait until you get here. You may see something we don't."

"I'll be there shortly. Thanks for the call, Mike." He hung up and stood. "Marge, I have to go to my cabin. It seems they found a dead woman in my back yard."

"Oh dear, could that be what you were feeling uneasy about this morning?"

Doyle thought about that, "Yeah, it could be. I'll be back when I can. Tell Oscar where I am and to keep an eye on the business."

"I will," she said as Doyle went out back to his car. He drove over to I-75 and headed up to his cabin.

He said to himself as he drove, "I hope it's no one I know."

*

Continued in the book…

Jim Richards series books by Bob Moats

(In series order)
Classmate Murders
Vegas Showgirl Murders
Dominatrix Murders
Mistress Murders
Bridezilla Murders
Magic Murders
Strip Club Murders
Made-for-TV Murders
Mystery Cruise Murders
Talk Show Murders
Sin City Murders
Black Widow Murders
Vegas Vigilante Murders
Area 51 Murders
Mortuary Murders
Hypnotic Murders
Sunshine State Murders
Blue Suede Murders
Honky Tonk Murders
Dark Carnival Murders
Lipstick Murders
Pasta Murders
Talent Show Murders
Shyster Murders
Campground Murders
Network Murders
Reunion Murders
Big Apple Murders
Kennel Murders
Trick or Treat Murders
Santa Murders
Wiseguy Murders

For a preview or to purchase a book, go to
http://murdernovels.com

What a few people are saying about the Jim Richards Murder Novels by Bob Moats

Mr. Moats, I just got your novel "Classmate Murders" and have to let you know, I read it in one evening. That is the first book I have ever done that with. That was the most enjoyable book I have ever read. I just started reading e-books, and reading again, after getting my wife a Kindle. This book was my 12th, and the best. I just got Las Vegas Showgirls to (read) tomorrow evening. I look forward to reading many of your books in this series. I have been searching for an author and books that were fun, entertaining reads. Your books are just the ticket.

Regards, A new fan, Bill from South Carolina

****

Hi Bob, I just had to write you... Last week I purchased a Nook Soft Touch e-reader. I was downloading free e-books and downloaded "Classmate Murders" from Barnes & Noble. I read it that night and enjoyed it so much that I went to search for the next one (as listed at end of the book). Read it and searched again. After reading the second one, I did a search from my e-reader for you and bought ALL of the books. So in the last week I have read all of the Jim Richards books. Finished the last one early this morning. I only read at night 10-6 when my neighbor is asleep. As I read the books I sometimes laughed and sometimes cried. I could relate to Jim as we are both in the 60s. I liked how "Jim" refers to previous murders in each book. That is great for anyone who has not read the books in order and also as fast as I did. Anyway, I just had to write and tell you how much I enjoyed the books.

Nancie S.

****

Another very nice comment submitted through my website from Micki P.:

"I recently was given a kindle for my 60th birthday. The first book I downloaded was the Classmate Murders and have now read every one of the them. Today I started on the Fatal Rejection series. Thank you for the wonderful ride with Jim and Penny and all the rest of the troop. I have laughed and giggled thru the stories, my poor family gave me the strangest looks! Now I really want a little Yorkie!! Fatal Rejection so far is another great read! I will be looking out for more of Jim Richards and since you are my #1 Author, anything of yours I can find."

Thank you for purchasing this book. I hope you enjoy it as much as I enjoyed writing it for my faithful readers. If you liked the book please feel free to write an honest review on the product page where you got this book from. I'd appreciate it. Please feel free to email me to tell me what you thought about my stories. I love hearing from the readers. I can be reached at murdernovels@bobmoats.com thanks again!